THE LONG SHADOW

also by Celia Fremlin

fiction

THE HOURS BEFORE DAWN

UNCLE PAUL

SEVEN LEAN YEARS

THE TROUBLE-MAKERS

THE JEALOUS ONE

PRISONER'S BASE

POSSESSION

APPOINTMENT WITH YESTERDAY

THE SPIDER-ORCHID

WITH NO CRYING

THE PARASITE PERSON

LISTENING IN THE DUSK

DANGEROUS THOUGHTS

ECHOING STONES

KING OF THE WORLD

short stories

DON'T GO TO SLEEP IN THE DARK

BY HORROR HAUNTED

A LOVELY DAY TO DIE

The
Long
Shadow

CELIA FREMLIN

faber

First published in 1975 by Gollancz
This edition first published in 2023 by Faber & Faber Ltd
The Bindery, 51 Hatton Garden
London ECIN 8HN

Typeset by Faber & Faber Ltd
Printed and bound by CPI Group (UK) Ltd, Croydon CRO 4YY

A CIP record for this book
is available from the British Library

ISBN 978-0-571-34810-7

2 4 6 8 10 9 7 5 3

I

'No, he died two months ago,' she said; 'I'm a widow,' and she waited for the tiny recoil behind his eyes, the twitch of unease, as he adjusted himself to the embarrassment of it. What *do* you say to middle-aged widows who turn up at parties so indecently soon? What do you talk to them *about*? Is the weather a safe topic? Or the state of the country?

I don't know either, Imogen wanted to scream at him. *I* don't know what you're supposed to say to me, or what I'm supposed to answer—or anything. This is the first time I've been anywhere since Ivor died, and I wish I'd never come, I wish I was safe at home being miserable. What a fool I was to let Myrtle persuade me, I might have known it would be like this . . . .

Myrtle wasn't really to blame, of course. Her intentions had been of the kindliest.

'It'll take you out of yourself, darling,' she'd insisted. 'After all, Ivor wouldn't have wanted you to go on grieving for ever . . . .'

*

Like hell he wouldn't! To Ivor's vast, irrepressible ego, for ever would have been all too short a tribute. He'd have loved to imagine that Imogen would grieve for him for ever, miss him for ever—indeed, that everyone else would, too: pupils, colleagues, neighbours; even his former wives and mistresses. All of them, all tearing their hair, rending their garments, flinging themselves on his pyre in an abandonment of grief. That's what Ivor would have liked, and Myrtle, of all people, must know it.

But of course, you couldn't expect her to mention it, any more than Imogen herself was mentioning it: and so, 'No, I suppose he wouldn't,' she'd lied, and had begun worrying about what to wear.

After all, it might be fun. It might, for a few hours, make her feel like a whole person again instead of the broken half of a couple.

It didn't, though; and it wasn't fun. By now, after nearly two hours of it, she felt not merely like a half person, but a half person who has been bisected vertically for an anatomical demonstration . . . all the raw, bleeding ends on display as the audience files past, each in turn peering with fascinated horror.

Over the rim of her glass, Imogen stole a look at her companion. Short, bearded, ten years younger than herself (as most men seemed to be these days)—already she could see the 'Let-me-out-of-this' signals flashing behind his horn-rimmed glasses. Any minute now. Myrtle (attentive hostess that she was) would be undulating along, all smiles, to mount yet another rescue operation. The fourth.

*

How long would it go on being like this? How long would the people she was introduced to stand in twitching silence, gulping back their opening gambits, washing their minds clear of funny stories? How long would she go on being an embarrassment and an obscenity wherever she went?

Embarrassment. Looking back over these past awful weeks, Imogen sometimes felt that the embarrassment had been worse than the grief: and there was no outlet for it in tears.

The hushed voices. The laughter that died as you drew near. The careful topics of conversation, picked clean of all reference to husbands, funerals, car accidents, professorships, love, happiness, unhappiness, men, women, life . . . . It didn't leave much.

*

Worst of all, perhaps, was the apparently unending procession of people who, incredibly, still hadn't heard, and had to be clobbered with the news in the first moment of meeting. Had to have the smiles slashed from their faces, the cheery words of greeting rammed back down their gullets as if by a gratuitous blow across the mouth. There they would be, waving from across the road, calling 'Hi!' from their garden gates, phoning by chance from Los Angeles, from Aberdeen, from Beckenham . . . . One and all to have their friendly overtures slammed into silence, their kindly voices choked with shock. One after another, day after day, over and over again: sometimes Imogen felt like the

Black Death stalking the earth, destroying everything in her path.

Just as, in a small way, she was destroying Myrtle's party right now, standing here in her bubble of darkness, grinning her death's-head grin, reaching out with black fingers to everyone who came near . . . .

Stop it, you fool! Stop it! Smile at him. Say something. As if he cares. You came, didn't you? You're Myrtle's guest, aren't you? Then do your bit . . . . Pull your weight . . . .

*

A heavier weight, of course, than heretofore. She was that hostess's nightmare now, an Extra Woman: and tonight, on top of being Extra, she wasn't even enjoying herself. Extra Women should enjoy themselves like mad, it's the least they can do.

'Lovely party, isn't it?' she yelled above the noise—and then checked herself. Maybe widows *shouldn't* be finding parties 'lovely'? Would this bearded person disapprove, think her heartless . . . ?

He was merely looking more frightened than ever: and, humiliating though it was, Imogen could not help being relieved to see Myrtle bearing down upon them, diamond earrings a-quiver, smile still in place.

'Darling, you *must* meet Terry,' she urged, steering Imogen with a light, steely hand away from her current victim and towards her new one. 'Terry's mad about Dutch Elm Disease, you know . . . . Terry, I want you to meet my great friend Imogen. She . . . she . . . .'

*

She's a widow, that's what she is. With wooden detachment, Imogen watched Myrtle's social aplomb faltering before the task of finding something intriguing to say about Imogen: something at least as amusing as Dutch Elm Disease.

She gave it up.

'Terry—Imogen. Imogen—Terry,' was finally the best she could do; and then retreated as if from the scene of the crime.

*

It was careers this time—Does your husband work at the University?—but it could just as easily have been holidays, or football, or Cordon Bleu cookery. There seemed to be no subject in the world, however seemingly innocuous, that didn't fetch up against your bereavement with a sickening thud in about two minutes flat. And it was worse than ever this time, for this Terry person was even younger than the others had been—a Ph.D. student, Imogen guessed, at the beginning of his first year—and correspondingly shy. So shy, indeed, and so socially inept, that he didn't merely twitch when he learned of Imogen's recent widowhood, he nearly jumped out of his skin. His head jerked backwards on his long, crimsoning neck, his wine slopped from his glass on to his trousers; bending to scrub them, he couldn't find his handkerchief; and Imogen, trying to come to the rescue, couldn't find hers either.

I must go, she thought, fumbling, with face averted, in her handbag, pretending to be still searching. I must go, I can't bear it here, I can't bear all these people. Ivor will be furious, he hates to leave parties early, but . . .

But Ivor is dead. Ivor neither knows nor cares what time you leave the party. He will never care again. You can leave exactly when you please.

Go on, then. Go right now, without even saying goodbye, and see who cares.

*

The quiet tree-lined roads that lay between Myrtle's home and Imogen's were almost deserted even at this comparatively early hour. It was a moonless night, heavy with moisture, and very still. Her feet, in their thin shoes, slithered among the drenched November leaves—slithered and skidded in the wet roadway just as Ivor's car must have done, on just such a night as this, as he drove—too fast, probably, and showing off for the benefit of any anonymous passer-by who might chance to be on the motorway at half past one in the morning. Showing off what his new car could do—what *he*, at nearly sixty, could still do. He, the ton-up Professor; immortal whizz-kid, beloved of Zeus, thus had he met his end.

It was barely ten o'clock when Imogen reached home, but the house, looming against the starless sky, was in darkness.

Well, of course it was. If you don't switch the lights on when you leave home in the bright afternoon, then they won't be on when you get back at night, will they?

But it hadn't always been like that. Not so long ago, lights had gone on as effortlessly in this house as the grass grows. Ivor never switched lights off, he hated that kind of cheeseparing frugality, and so by now, by ten o'clock, there would once have been a blaze of light from every window, the tall house lit like an ocean liner ploughing through the night sky, with Ivor on board.

Imogen shivered. As she pushed open the garden gate, a little scutter of drops from the overhanging bushes flicked over her hair and shoulders. In the darkness under the porch, she fumbled for her key, found it, fitted it into the front door. Then, with a tiny bracing of the nerves, like a bather stepping down into icy water, she pushed open the door and went inside.

*

They had all gone now: the relations, the lawyers, the neighbours, the family friends. Even her stepdaughter Dot, child of Ivor's first marriage, had gone; she had left this morning. Left properly, that is, after eight weeks of commuting back and forth between her own home and Imogen's in a delightful whirl of conflicting duties. Dot liked duties, they made her feel secure and indispensable; and conflicting duties were the best of all, putting her straight into the spiritually-propertied classes, a sort of emotional tycoon, needed and wanted everywhere. Even Herbert, her husband, started wanting her when she'd been away long enough for the house to get in a real mess and for the little boys, Vernon and Timmie, to have no clean clothes to go to school in. 'When are you coming back, Dot?' he'd say, reluctantly pleading: and then, no sooner had she been home for a day or two, and the family beginning to take her for granted again, than she remembered how much her stepmother still needed her, how indispensable she was for sorting her father's things.

'I remember *that*: that's Mother's,' she'd say, in hushed, almost religious tones, scooping up this or that as she stalked eagle-eyed round the house. Or, 'Aunt Bertha gave him those; I feel sure she'd have wished them to stay on our side of the family.'

'Shouldn't Robin be getting some of them?' was the only objection Imogen had raised to Dot's simple system of allocation; and Dot had replied, with some asperity, that if her young brother wanted a finger in the pie, then he should turn up occasionally and help with things, instead of disappearing straight after the funeral and not even bothering to write.

Fair enough. But Robin was like that, she hadn't expected to see much of him. From now on, she wouldn't be seeing much of Dot, either; the sixty-odd miles to and fro to London from here were a lot, now that the main crisis was over. The neighbours were thinning out, too; they had been wonderful, all of them, at the beginning, telephoning and calling at the house to ask if there was anything they could do. During those first days, kindness had hit the house like a tornado, but now, at last, the flood was receding: the storm-centre of benevolence had moved on, away from this house, somewhere else. Even Edith Hartman from next door had at last stopped popping in with cups of tepid Oxo and soothing stories about people who had died of cancer recently.

Tonight, for the first time, Imogen was going to be absolutely alone. For nearly a minute, after closing the front door behind her, she stood quite still in the pitch dark and the silence, waiting for loneliness to strike. It was like waiting, when you have stubbed your toe against a rock, for the pain to begin.

*

She felt nothing but an overpowering thankfulness. Peace at last! The voices, the luggage, the bedlam of comings and goings; the tears, the mealtimes, the arguments—they were all over. Silence, solitude and peace were at last to be hers.

And Ivor. There was room for Ivor again, now that everyone was gone. When she had taken off her coat, and changed from her teetering party shoes into soft slippers, she set off on a tour of the house, trying to recapture him. Room by room she wandered through her empty home looking at things: touching his books, his desk, his great leather armchair, and sniffing at the heavy bronze ash-tray where the ash from his pipe still lingered: cold as his own ashes, and almost exactly the same age. And as she padded across the carpets, and over the rich, exotic rugs that he had brought home like the spoils of war from all over the world, she felt as if it was she who was the one who was dead; the ghost returning to its old haunts. Her feet, as she moved, made scarcely as much noise as the autumn leaves outside.

The kitchen, clean and gleaming, as Dot had left it this morning. The drawing-room, already like a museum with disuse and with the weeks of hushed voices and solemn deliberations. The dining-room, no longer the scene of candle-lit dinner parties for Ivor's important friends, but become a sort of office, the headquarters for the business side of grief. The long

refectory table was piled high with the letters of sympathy, condolence and eulogy that had come in from all over the world.

*

How Ivor would have loved being dead! It was a shame that he
was missing it all. How he would have loved to watch the letters
pouring in, day after day, by every post, in their tens and in their
dozens, each one a tribute to himself. Imogen pictured him gathering them up in handfuls off the mat, pretending indifference.
'I'll have a look at this stuff later,' he'd have said, elaborately
off-hand; and then, secretive as an alcoholic, he'd have slipped off
with them into his study. And once inside, with the door closed,
how he would have fastened on them, face alight, unable to tear
them open fast enough . . . .

'. . . Such a friend as I know I shall never find again . . .'

'. . . a great scholar, and yet deeply humble . . .'

'. . . It is his courage that I shall always remember, his courage and high spirits. I'll never forget that evening, with darkness
already falling, and the camels still hadn't arrived . . .'

'The best lecturer we have ever had, and the most kindly of
men. His concern for his students was unfailing . . . an inspiration to the brilliant . . . a pillar of strength to the weak . . .
a great scholar and a great teacher . . . a loyal and much-loved
colleague . . .'

'. . . I'll never forget his kindness to me that day . . . I a shy,
insignificant first-year student, and he already world-famous in
his field . . . . He didn't say much, just sat there, smoking his
pipe, letting me talk . . . but it was exactly what I needed . . .'

Slowly, Imogen folded the last letter, laid it back on the pile with the rest. These, then, were Ivor's memorials: golden memories engraved upon a thousand hearts: outpourings of admiration and of love from all over the world. This was what was left of him.

And somewhere beneath it all, buried deeper than in the deepest grave, lay the real man.

A sense of loss, total and irretrievable, overwhelmed her, and laying her head down among the scattered papers, she felt her cheeks soaked in tears.

'Oh, God,' she murmured—and this was the nearest thing to prayer that Imogen had ever uttered—'Please God, don't let me ever forget what a bastard he could be.'

2

It was the grandfather clock striking midnight that roused her.

She should be writing answers to these letters, not crying over them. In two whole months, she and Dot between them had answered barely a third; and they were still coming in.

'Ten a day,' Dot had proposed, in the heavy-handed, no-nonsense style that had kept her husband working late for years. 'If we each answer ten a day, Imogen, then they'll be done in— let's see. Twenty a day is a hundred and forty a week . . . that's a month, then. Just over a month . . . .'

Soon, though, it began to appear that *five* a day might have been a more realistic target . . . then three . . . and then two; and at this point the actuarial calculations became so depressing— the whole thing extending, it seemed, over the best part of both their lifetimes—that Dot decided that what was needed was a System. Hence the in-trays, and the cardboard boxes, and the slips of paper saying things like 'To be answered before Dec. 7th'; or 'Friends, current'; 'Friends, Miscellaneous'; 'Publishers etc., except for Charlie'; and 'The Australian Lot'. Imogen found the principle of classification beyond her; but she could see that it was easier than actually writing the letters.

In the last resort, there is only one way of getting something done, and that is to do it. This was something you couldn't really explain to Dot. She took after her mother, Ivor always used to say; which may or may not have been true. In all these years, Imogen had never actually met this earliest one of her predecessors, and so these paternal accusations were hard to assess.

Rubbing her eyes, still stiff and sore with crying, Imogen reached out blindly for the topmost letter of the nearest pile. 'Take the one nearest you', they always used to say when you were a child at the tea-table; and really it was good advice. Whatever this topmost letter was, important or unimportant, easy or difficult, urgent or otherwise, she would answer it—just simply answer it—here and now. Thus would be removed the awful burden of deciding where to start.

*

It *would* be this one! Well, wouldn't it?—and no more than you deserve, my girl, leaving the thing to Fate like that. And you the wife of a Classics Professor, too—all those Greek plays. You, of all women, should know the kind of thing Fate gets up to when the Gods are no longer on your side . . . .

The *widow* of a Classics Professor, she corrected herself; and began to read. Twice, and then a third time, she read through the five closely-written pages; and then stared, for nearly a minute, at the heavy velvet curtains that shut out the night beyond the big windows.

At last, drawing the writing-pad towards her, she picked up her pen.

'Dear Cynthia,' should she say, or 'Dear Mrs Barnicott'? What *do* you call your husband's ex-wife—the second one—who in thirteen years has scarcely exchanged a word with you? Riffling back through the blue airmail pages, Imogen sought some clue to the etiquette of the thing, but there was none.

'My dear—' the letter had started; 'My dear, words cannot express . . .'

A good reason, one might have thought, for using fewer of them. Five *pages*!

Still, here goes . . . .

She had intended it to be a short letter: short and dignified, and in as marked a contrast as possible to Cynthia's own maundering hyperbole. But now here she was, herself, already on her third page, and still with almost everything to explain—or to avoid explaining.

'No, of course I don't find it strange that you should still love him,' she wrote, 'and I'm sure that in his heart of hearts he knew you did . . . .'

Of course he knew, the old so-and-so. Knew it, and gloried in it, as he gloried in anybody's love, any time. He just didn't want to have to bother about it, that was all; and of course, with ex-wives there was the money thing, too, complicating the nostalgic glow he'd have liked to have felt about them.

'. . . As you say, some decision will have to be reached about the continuance of your alimony,' wrote Imogen rapidly, as if the issue would dissipate itself into thin air if only she set it down fast enough: '. . . I am sure the Executors have the matter in hand, and you will be hearing from them shortly . . . .'

You should be so lucky! 'Shortly', indeed. It'll take months and months, money things always do, as you, dear, should know better than anyone. How many years was it before you finally got Ivor pinned down over the maintenance?—Five years?—Seven? Nearly half of *my* married life with him, anyway. If you knew what he used to *say* about you, dear, at breakfast time, which was when your nagging letters mostly arrived. I used to watch the nice crisp bacon I'd cooked congealing on his plate, and the perfectly-fried egg chilling to leather . . . . And now you have the cheek to write me a letter of condolence.

Oh, well. On we go.

'. . . While I do understand how you feel, I don't really think that any purpose would be served by your coming to England just now (My God, I'll kill her!), and although I appreciate, and am moved by, your suggestion that Ivor would have liked us to mourn his loss together . . .'

Yes. It would have been rather Ivor's thing: his wife and his ex-wife sobbing broken-heartedly together over his demise. Maybe Number One would like to come along, too, from her Home for Inebriates or whatever, and make up a threesome?

O.K., so Ivor would have liked it. But then he won't be here, will he, dear? It's whether I like it that counts now, *I'm* the one who'll have to meet you at the airport, put clean sheets on your bed, ask you if you'd like hot-water-bottles, cocoa, cornflakes . . . . And then there you'll still be, next day, and I'll have to talk to you, pass you the marmalade, think what the hell to do with you. And you're bound to want to stay for weeks and weeks, coming all the way from Bermuda, £400 return, isn't it?

It isn't that I hate you, dear, it's just that I don't want to have to bother about you. Just like Ivor . . . .

*

Just like Ivor. How Ivor would have laughed if he could have known of the wicked asides that kept coming into her head while she wrote her correct and decorous letter. She imagined the low rumble of laughter as he leaned over her shoulder, reading what she had written. She seemed to hear his rich, mocking voice suggesting outrageous postscripts and addenda:

'Send her a row of kisses from me,' he'd have said, in the special jeering voice that he reserved for making reference to his former wives. 'She won't know, will she, that "X" is the ideogram for "Get lost" in Old Akkadian. Look—like this—it represents a falling man being thrust away over the threshold . . . .'

How they'd have laughed over it together, she and Ivor—might, indeed, have actually put the row of X's, giggling like schoolchildren as he egged her on. Jeering at his ex-wives was something that Ivor and Imogen loved to do together, they were so good at it: it was like one of those brilliant ballroom-dancing partnerships. Somehow, it brought them very close.

Never again. She could never be funny and wicked like this with anyone but Ivor. Funny, outrageous, in fits of heartless laughter, ruthless with love . . . .

Hell, she was crying again! She was sick to death of crying, and here it was starting all over again, the tears dripping soppily down on to the letter making it look all blotched and pathetic.

Stop it, you fool, stop it!

Pathetic. A pity Cynthia couldn't be here watching, it would have warmed the cockles of her cliché-ridden little heart. The poor lonely widow, sitting in her empty home long after midnight, sobbing her heart out over stupid jokes that nobody would ever find funny again.

*

It was perhaps half an hour later—somewhere between one and two o'clock in the morning—when the telephone began to ring: and at first Imogen, in a stupor that was half misery and half sleep, fancied that it was morning: that she had overslept, allowing the bustle and clamour of the day to get ahead of her—doorbells, telephones, laundry-men, neighbours. She made as if to leap out of bed—and only then discovered that she wasn't *in* bed. Had, in fact, never gone to bed at all last night . . . Lord, it still *was* last night . . . !

Sitting up writing letters . . . . Yes, that was it. The unfinished letter to Cynthia still lay in front of her on the table . . . .

Ring-ring . . . Ring-ring . . . on and on. Who could it be, ringing at such an hour? And with what sort of news to impart? Imogen wasn't afraid of bad news as a normal person is afraid. She felt immunised by grief from any further grief, and so she picked up the receiver without a tremor—with scarcely a twinge of curiosity, even. If they had said, 'Your sister in Australia is dead', or 'Your stepdaughter Dot is dead', or 'Your stepson Robin', or one of the grandchildren—she would just have said 'Yes, I know'.

It was something of a shock, though, when they didn't say any of these things. It made it hard to concentrate. 'Mrs Barnicott?' the voice kept saying, 'That *is* Mrs Barnicott, isn't it?'

A man's voice. A young man—no, a boy, really . . . and as he went on talking, Imogen's mind gradually began to clear.

'At the party . . . ?' Of course. Myrtle's party. That dreadful party last night—tonight—this evening—whenever it was. Who, though . . . ?

'Yes . . . of course I remember . . .' she hazarded, playing for time: and then, suddenly, she *did* remember, and her voice stiffened with embarrassment as it all came back to her.

'You're—we were talking about Dutch Elm Disease?' she ventured, guardedly.

'No, actually.'

Unhelpful, but factually correct. It was Myrtle, not he, who had said that he was interested in Dutch Elm Disease. Mad about it, she'd said.

Imogen tried again.

'You're—you're Terry, aren't you?' she said, pulling the name out of the medley of her recollections. 'You're—'

'No, actually,' he said again, and this time even more unhelpfully. 'The name is "Teri", T-E-R-I . . .'

'Oh.' The amendment, it seemed to Imogen, provided singularly little opening for further conversation. 'I hope your trousers were all right?' she floundered on, inanely—but the whole thing seemed so insane, and especially at this time of night—'The wine, I mean . . .'

What an idiotic conversation! People had no *right* to make you behave so idiotically.

'Yes. They're O.K.'

Deadlock once more. Imogen could hear his breath gathering itself together as whatever it was he'd really rung up about came thrusting upwards towards his vocal chords.

'Look, Mrs Barnicott, what I wanted to tell you . . . That is, I wanted to apologise, actually. I mean, the way I freaked . . . the wine and that. I'm sorry . . .'

'That's all right,' said Imogen, a trifle frostily. Why couldn't he leave the unfortunate incident alone?

'You see,' he was continuing—making matters worse with every syllable—'it was a shock, you see, when you told me that your husband was—that is, when I realised you were—'

A widow. O.K., O.K. Did the young fool imagine that she didn't *know* which was the word that had thrown him? Of course he'd been shocked, everyone was. But did he need to ring up at two in the morning to say so?

She braced herself against his pity as against the recoil of a swing-door. The pity of the unscathed young is the worst of all.

'Yes, I'm afraid—' she was beginning, cold and retaliatory—and then, suddenly, she realised that her caller was still speaking.

'You see,' he was saying, 'I hadn't realised who you were at first—Myrtle introduced us by our Christian names only, if you remember, and of course it didn't convey anything to me. It was when you told me your *other* name, and who your husband was—that's what threw me. You see, Mrs Barnicott, it just happens that I know rather a lot about your husband, and about the circumstances of his death. And one of the things I know is that his death wasn't an accident. And you know it too, Mrs Barnicott: you know it better than anyone, because you killed him.'

3

A nut, of course. With shaking hands, Imogen listened in horror. The sort of nut who gets his pleasure from kicking those who are down: who thinks it is fun to make an already despairing widow feel even worse.

Only as it happened he hadn't made her feel worse. He had made her feel much, much better. At the words 'You killed him!' a shaft of incredible, singing happiness had gone through her—a sensation more shocking and more inexplicable even than the accusation itself. For one dazzling, lurid second she was no longer a dreary, pitiable widow, but a glittering monster of wickedness. Come along, dear, I'd like you to meet my friend the murderess. Let them gape and stutter over *that* for a change. Let them gasp, and spill red wine down themselves, out of fear instead of pity. 'Widow', indeed.

Clutching the telephone to her ear, the crazy accusation still ringing inside her skull, Imogen was filled with a dizzying sense of change, of hope, of the Outside. There it still was, the crazy, hazardous, unpredictable Outside, just as it used to be, with its nut-cases, its enormities, its random bolts from the blue. This grey capsule of bereavement, in which she had been existing all these weeks as in a padded cell, was not all that was left upon the earth after all. Somewhere beyond its walls the silly old real world was still spinning. For one brief moment, it had been vouchsafed to her to hear again the whistle of its slings and arrows, to feel again the thrust and knobbiness of its muddled burdens.

The moment was gone almost before she knew it. She was back in the capsule again: crying again.

'A nut-case,' she sobbed angrily, slamming down the receiver. 'As if everything wasn't bloody enough—a bloody nut-case!'

*

'A nut-case,' Edith-next-door confirmed, pursing her lips over sweet, strong coffee the next morning, and nodding darkly at her neighbour who was now sitting, meek and bereaved, across the hearth from her—across what would have been the hearth, that is to say, if Edith's home hadn't been central heated throughout, with plastic daffodils and mummified grasses where flames had once leaped and flickered. It was ridiculously early for coffee really, only just after breakfast, but Edith liked her troubles fresh, and so the moment she realised that something new was amiss in the House of Mourning (which was how she currently described her next-door-neighbour's home), she had raced for phone, coffee-pot and kettle in almost a single practised movement.

'You want to watch out for this sort of thing,' she was now advising Imogen, scooping sugar from the bottom of her cup with a sort of ladylike intensity of greed, and conveying, some-how, the impression that she had just been proved right about something. 'You can't be too careful, my dear . . . a woman on her own . . . lonely . . . unprotected. *I* should know. Do you realise, Imogen, that it's been four years—four whole years!—since my dear Desmond passed on? Four years next Thursday . . . ?'

This four years' seniority in widowhood was something that Edith rather harped on, it seemed to Imogen. She brought it into almost every conversation, sometimes to comfort, sometimes to warn, and sometimes to hint, very gently, that Imogen herself wasn't grieving quite enough.

'You're so *brave*,' she would say, 'and after only two months, too. Why, after two months I could do nothing but cry and cry. But you know, dear'—here she would start dabbing at her own eyes, peering sharply past the handkerchief to see if Imogen was dabbing too—'you know, don't you, that there's no need to keep a stiff-upper-lip with *me*. Go on—don't bottle it up—have a good cry. Remember, I've been through it myself, I know just what you're feeling.'

You don't, though, Imogen would think sullenly. If you did you'd shut up, shut up, shut up, *shut up!* While aloud, 'Yes, Edith, I know,' she'd prevaricate, docile, and dimly guilty, and unable to summon up a single tear. And the funny thing is, she sometimes mused, your upper lip really *does* feel stiff.

But this morning, Edith was too much interested in the story she had just heard to bother with the etiquette of sorrow. She was full of advice and timely warnings.

'. . . Can't be too careful,' she was repeating, knowledgeable and slightly competitive. '*I* used to get calls like that all the time. Every night for months: and sometimes in the day as well. Oh, it was terrible!'

Naturally. Everything—every goddam bloody thing—had been just that little bit more terrible for Edith than it now was for Imogen. Aware of inferior status in the complex hierarchy of bereavement, Imogen bowed her head over her coffee. Whatever it took to get calls 'like that' every night and sometimes in the day as well, she, Imogen, clearly hadn't got it. *She* had had only *one* call 'like that' in eight weeks.

Like what, anyway? A spark of fight stirred in her, and she raised her head.

'They accused you of murdering Desmond? *Every night?*' she inquired innocently—and as she spoke, the sense of Ivor not being there—not listening, not knowing, not being amused— went through her like a sword-thrust. He'd always loved to take the mickey out of Edith-next-door, or to hear that Imogen had done so. Telling him about it afterwards had been part of the fun. From now on, if she cared to score off Edith, she'd be scoring alone.

'Imogen! What a terrible thing to say! *Of course* no one ever accused me of . . . of . . . What an idea! My own darling husband . . . so close we were . . . such companions . . . never a cross word . . .'

Ivor's assorted cross words lashed across the conversation like the crack of a whip, and both women were struck silent for a moment, listening to them over the years. Booming across summer lawns . . . resounding from the frozen garage . . . reverberating loud and clear from landing windows. Where the hell's my this? Who's been using my that? Why the hell can't you ever . . . ? For four years, ever since she moved in next door, Edith must have been listening to this sort of thing over the hedge, storing it up.

It wasn't *fair*. Ivor had been *alive*, dammit, all those years, whereas Darling Desmond had been safely dead. How can a live man possibly compete in patience and long-suffering with a dead one? Darling Desmond held all the aces, there under the green grass of the churchyard, smooth and lush by now, four years established, and perhaps with daisies growing. *His* cross words, whatever they may have been, were buried with him, and there would be no resurrection.

Hell and damnation! The half-suppressed sniffs, the gulping sounds from behind Edith's poised handkerchief, warned Imogen that she'd done it again. She'd allowed the conversation to work round to Darling Desmond, and now here was Edith crying about him all over again.

Most crying is not only *about* someone, it is also *at* someone; and Edith's was no exception. She was crying at Imogen, right on target. Look, the sobs and sniffles were saying, as plain as you please, look how *I'm* weeping for *my* dear husband after four whole years! Whereas *you*, after only two months . . . Parties . . . Hair-dos . . . Look at me, Imogen! Look! Real tears!

But Imogen wouldn't look.

I won't play, she was saying to herself, I'm keeping out of the game, I'm not competing. Let her win.

But *was* it a game? For one sick, terrible moment there flashed across Imogen's mind the awful possibility that Edith's ostentatious tears might, after all, be genuine? She might, after all this time, be truly still grieving? Look, ran this new and terrifying message, look, after four whole years you still *do* feel like this. You really do.

I won't, said Imogen to herself, squeezing her eyes tight shut

25

and clenching her fists in a strange, savage kind of prayer. I won't, I won't, I won't. Not for *four years*!

*

'And this is why I understand so well how you are feeling, dear,' Edith was concluding, blowing her nose and scrubbing at her red eyes. 'You might think, perhaps, that by now I'd have begun to get over it . . . to forget. But believe me, dear, it isn't so. The grief is as vivid to me now as on the day he died . . . .'

Vivider, probably. You don't really remember much of that first day, and what you do remember has very little to do with grief. A tap dripping. A porridge-saucepan soaking in the sink—for the last time, as it happens, because he was the only one who liked porridge; but this hasn't occurred to you yet. The dawn lightens beyond the windows; it is morning, full day. There seems to be nothing to do, and so naturally you don't do anything. The biggest non-event of a lifetime.

Had it been different for Edith, that first day of hers without Darling Desmond? Or is it, perhaps, the case that the weeks, and the months, and the years are all the time adding, by stealth, and little by little, every bit as much to a memory as they take away? Until, at last, the things that didn't happen have grown like moss over the things that did; a soft green cushion on which the mind can rest at last?

What sort of things would she, herself, be remembering about Ivor, and her grief for him, after four long years? What kind of a man would he appear to her to have been, once four summers lay between them, four grey and harassing winters; four holidays, perhaps? And all the new people— new friends, new neighbours, new window-cleaners, who had never known him? Beyond the lengthening barrier of the years, ever smaller, ever further away, what would Ivor's tiny, wildly-gesticulating figure look like when she tried to hold it in her fast-receding gaze?

Not like Darling Desmond, anyway. On this, at least, she was resolved.

'He used to get into the most awful tempers,' she said to Edith, loudly and suddenly, and apropos of nothing. 'The tiniest thing—one of the ivory chess-pieces out of its box—or if I forgot to order the peat for the roses . . . .'

Edith stared, her mouth opening and shutting silently, while she sought vainly among her habitual repertoire of reactions for something that would do. There was nothing; and so she settled, at last, for being vaguely offended. Not that Imogen's outburst had been an insult, exactly, but it was— well—ungrateful, in some complicated way. After all, if she, Edith, was prepared to understand so well how Imogen was feeling, then surely Imogen could at least go to the trouble of feeling that way?

'You're overwrought, dear,' Edith diagnosed warily. 'You've been doing too much. Why don't you go and have a nice lie-down?'

Nice lie-downs were almost everyone's remedy, when the strain of Imogen's bereavement became too much for them. She couldn't really blame them—bereavement is so non-stop, it never lets up; people have to have a bit of time off from it. And let's face it, if you aren't lying on your bed, then where *are* you? Somewhere else, of course; it gets on people's nerves, after a while.

*

This, really, was the wonderful thing about having the house to herself at last: she was on nobody's nerves. How wonderful to be able to saunter up the stairs, and down again, in and out of the kitchen, without anyone saying What are you looking for, dear? What do you want, dear? Do you mind getting your feet off my nerves, dear?

You don't want anything, that's the whole trouble. You *want* to want things again, in fact you wander about trying to find something to want—a newspaper, perhaps; some half-finished knitting; an orange. You don't really want these things, but all the same there is a faint vestigial stirring of discontent when you find the oranges are all gone. Better than nothing.

Back into the kitchen again. Open the door of the fridge, and stare in, and wonder, supposing you were hungry, what would you actually want for lunch?

Not pâté, anyway. Jars and jars of it, all brought by nice people who wanted to give something a little more practical than flowers, and not as heartless as theatre tickets.

'Delicious!' Dot had said, reprovingly, storing the fourth jar away with the rest at the back of the fridge, 'and so kind of them.' But *she* hadn't eaten any of it, either.

Out of the kitchen, then, and up the softly-carpeted stairs. How lovely to steal about like this, without purpose, and with no one demanding your reasons! To drift from room to room:

to stand vacantly, for minutes on end, at the bedroom window, staring down at the sodden lawn where Ivor's barrow of dead leaves still stood, unemptied, just where he had left it that last afternoon. For two months it had waited, silently grinding its wooden feet deeper and deeper into the wet turf as the weeks went by. By spring, there would be neat, dead little rectangles of impacted earth among the new, tender grass, unless someone moved the barrow, and of course no one would.

How lovely to stare, unperturbed, at the slow decay of things, with no one at your elbow saying don't brood, dear, don't worry, dear, everything'll be all right, dear, just relax, dear, and if you leave it out there much longer, dear, it'll rot.

Well, of course it will. Do you think widows don't know about Entropy? They know better than anyone, actually, even the ones who have never heard of the word.

How lovely not to be watched and worried over. To be able to sit hunched on the edge of the big double bed, your face empty, your jaw slack, and no one coming in and saying Are you all right, dear? To be able to kick your shoes off, to walk on tip-toe for no particular reason, feeling the thick pile of the carpet Ivor had spent two hundred pounds on between your toes. To make faces at yourself in the long mirror, tongue lolling, nose all scrunched up, eyes pushed up at the corner like a mongol. Yah, you ugly creature! You hideous, miserable creature, Yah!

'Step! I say, Step, whatever *are* you doing?'

In utter confusion, her face a kaleidoscope of hastily-reassembled features, Imogen whirled round.

'Robin!' she cried, half-laughing in her shock and embarrass-ment, 'What on earth . . . ? I thought you were in Yorkshire . . . ?'

29

'Do you often practice for beauty-competitions when you're on your own?' Robin enquired with interest, moving forward into the room to give his stepmother a perfunctory hug. Then, holding her away from him: 'What's the matter. Step? Aren't you pleased to see me?'

Imogen looked up at her stepson warily. A six-footer like his father; and broad with it: but there the resemblance ended. Instead of Ivor's shaggy lion's mane, Robin's hair was dark and straight and smooth, and already thinning on top. The heavy shoulders, powerful and bull-like in the father, made the son look merely overweight. Although he was only a year or two past thirty, his body was already running to fat—and at these tiny, preliminary signs of future middle-age, Imogen felt a little twinge of sadness, as at a fresh, tiny bereavement.

His face, though, was as boyish as ever—rosy, beaming, and imperturbable, just as it had been when Imogen had first met him, nearly twelve years ago: she a nervous, strung-up prospective stepmother, he an amused, unruffled, infinitely tolerant undergraduate in his second year.

'I'm going to call you "Step",' he'd informed her, after a careful scrutiny (so it seemed to Imogen) of her every inadequacy, from her flushed face and wilting hair (it had been July, and a heatwave) to her white pointed shoes that hurt, and were already smudged with green from the immemorial lawns across which Ivor was privileged, as a Senior Member, to walk, and to escort her, introducing her to the glories and honours of his status in the University.

'Step'—Robin tried out the word experimentally, and nodded. 'Is that O.K. with you? This way, you see, we bypass the

Mummy-Mother-or-Ma thing. And since I've already got a Mummy, a Mother, and a Ma . . .'

Imogen saw his point, and smiled; and from that moment a firm friendship sprung up between them which had withstood, somehow, eleven years of almost non-stop family rows.

For Ivor's charm, so potent in the world at large, seemed to be brought up short as against a brick wall when it came to dealing with his own son. Impervious to blandishments, unperturbed by rage, Robin had seemed to take a delight, from his earliest years, in annoying his father to the limit, and then getting out from under just before the explosion. Some-one else, of course, was left to take the brunt of it—usually Imogen.

'Robin, why do you *do* it?' Imogen had once protested—it was when Robin had chucked his Dip. Ed. in the middle of the second term, and had then turned up at home, carefree as springtime, to borrow money.

'It seems they won't keep on my grant, now I'm not there,' he'd explained, aggrievedly; and then, while the house rocked to the repercussions of this remark, he'd slipped out to the garden shed to tinker with his bicycle. Imogen found him there, an hour later, eating Coxes from the apple-racks, and reading *Private Eye*.

'Why can't you at least be more *tactful*?' she'd pleaded with him. 'It's as if you're *trying* to madden him. Why do you *do* it?'

A reasonable question: but Robin had just given a little laugh.

'Like father, like son,' he'd said lightly, through a mouthful of apple: and Imogen had been left to conclude that he was joking. For what could possibly be found in common between Ivor's sky-ride to glory in the University firmament and Robin's aimless teetering from one failure to another on the lowest rungs of the academic ladder?

Anyway, that's what he'd said; and then, while all hell still raged at home, he'd cycled quietly away to wheedle the required sum out of his sister Dot, and had vanished with it to Istanbul for months and months. By the time he reappeared, there was so much else that was new, and worse, for his father to be angry about, that the original misdemeanour quite faded from recollection.

This had always been the pattern: as Robin's current tiresomeness escalated, so did the past tend to get forgiven. Or perhaps not so much forgiven as wearily obliterated: the day came, at last, when Imogen realised that the battle of father and son was over: Ivor no longer cared. After all, success was by now coming to him from so many directions that he hardly needed a successful son as well. And anyway, Imogen told herself, you can't go on worrying for ever. By the time delinquent sons are nearing thirty, most parents have surely given up trying to be proud of them, and are merely thankful that they are still alive—if they are—and that all the things that almost happened to them, didn't.

And now Ivor was dead: and here was Robin, smiling, as if butter wouldn't melt in his mouth, his same old nineteen-year-old smile (or almost): and asking her, reproachfully, if she wasn't pleased to see him?

'Is it some girl?' she asked him warily. 'Or is it money? You do realise, don't you, dear, that until we get Probate . . .'

'*Step!* You mercenary old monster! As if I'd mention the sordid subject of money "at a time like this"—as your precious Edith-next-door would put it! Honestly, Step, you must think I have a heart of stone! Right first time—I have. But all the same, it's not money. Not this time. What I was wondering, Step dear, is whether it wouldn't be a good idea, now that Dad's popped it, for me to come back and live at home? What think you, Step? Good idea? Yes?'

4

The question mark in his voice was phoney. He wasn't asking her, he was telling her. So sure was he of being able to twist her round his little finger he hardly bothered to do it any more. There he stood, beaming, utterly satisfied with himself, and waiting for her little cries of rapture.

'I shan't actually *be* here,' he continued, a shade less confidently, when she didn't answer. 'I'll be taking off almost at once, as a matter of fact, for maybe Sardinia. Or there's a chap I know in Spain who runs a ceramics factory . . . . It's just that it seems silly to keep on the flat when . . .'

'You've lost your job, you mean?' interposed Imogen resignedly. 'They sacked you, I suppose, these Fertiliser people . . . ?'

'They did not! I wish you'd try to summon up a bit of faith in me, Step, just now and again. I sacked *them*, as a matter of fact. I just wasn't going to stand for . . .'

Here it came again. Yet another lot of antedeluvian directors, obsessed with paper qualifications: yet another blinkered has-been of a firm, blind as always to their own best interests in the matter of retaining on their payroll this incomparable, this irreplaceable employee, who could have put everything to rights, from top management to office-boy, and have set their export figures soaring, if only he could have managed to get up in the morning.

*

Unemployed. Idling around the house all day. Eating. Borrowing the air-fare to Sardinia. Or Spain, as the case might be. Coming back penniless, and slightly ill, and with mountains of luggage to clutter up the house. On the other hand . . .

'I don't know, Robin, I'm sure,' she began, trying to sound as if the decision was at least partly in her hands and not his. 'I don't want to be rushed into anything. Everyone's been on at me, what am I going to do about the house . . . I might sell it,' she finished, on a little spurt of defiance.

'You won't, though,' predicted Robin, flopping down on the big bed (without removing his shoes, as always) and arranging the pillows under his head, 'widows never do. They *talk* about it, yes, endlessly. For the first six months, they give you the "I-can't-stand-the-memories" bit, non-stop. They can afford to, you see, at this stage, because no one is so hard-hearted as to expect the poor grieving creatures to *do* anything. But then, when recovery looms, and they are confronted with the sheer bloody bother of actually moving, then they drop the memories thing like a hot brick, and instead they decide that they can't bear to leave the rhubarb that *He* planted, or whatever. That's why I won't have anything to do with them, I stick to divorcees . . .'

At these words, Imogen was struck by a new and appalling possibility.

35

'Margot!' she exclaimed. 'What about Margot? You're not planning to bring *her* here, are you?'

'Margot? Good God, no! That's all over. Didn't I tell you, her mother wouldn't keep the kid any longer: and so that was that.' He paused; and when Imogen remained silent, he continued, a little defensively: 'Everyone has their breaking point, Step. Mine's kids. I told you.'

Ivor's grandchild, was he talking about? Or just any old unimportant baby, the offspring merely of Margot and some unknown man? Imogen had never dared to ask: nor did she dare now. There was no point: there'd be nothing she could do. She'd never liked this Margot woman anyway; a predatory creature with coarse skin—just what Robin deserved, no doubt; but she was glad, all the same, that he wasn't getting her.

Forget the baby, then, dark and yellow like its mother, and a slow talker into the bargain—almost two, and with barely a dozen words at its command. Change the subject, quickly.

'Oh, Robin, such an extraordinary thing!' she burst out, perhaps a little too exuberantly, and over-effusive: 'I must tell you! There was this extraordinary young man, you see, I met him at Myrtle's party, and what does he do afterwards but phone me up at two in the morning to say . . .'

She laughed, and stumbled, and fell over her words as she recounted last night's adventure: not sure whether she was telling a funny story or confiding a problem. Robin hitched himself higher on the pillows as he listened, and lit a cigarette. At the end, he nodded gravely.

'I didn't know you had it in you, Step,' he commented. 'But

tell me—how did you get away with it? Don't the police suspect anything . . . ?'

'*Robin!*' She hurled a cushion across the room at him, sharply and dead straight—though whether in fun or in genuine outrage, she couldn't for the life of her have said.

'That's right, set the house on fire as well,' he remarked equably, bending down to retrieve the cigarette that had been hurled from his fingers, and had landed, still smouldering, under the bed. 'But go on, Step, tell me some more. This chap with Dutch Elm Disease—what's his name?'

'. . . a *thesis* on Dutch Elm Disease,' Imogen interposed, giggling—it was the first giggle of her widowhood, and it felt strange—'His name's "Teri", believe it or not. Not "Terry". "Teri", with an "i".'

'He accused you of *murder*? This Teri . . . ?'

'Why—yes—' Imogen looked at her stepson in sudden unease. Murder was a serious subject, surely?—why wasn't he laughing? 'What is it, Robin? What's the matter? Do you know him, or something?'

Thankfully, she heard the bantering tone return to his voice:

'Know him? *Really*, Step. I don't have to consort with these loons and goons, why should I? I only got a Third, remember? It's the First-Class brains that addle, not the Thirds.'

He paused, and once again appeared to be thinking more deeply than was quite natural.

'What did you tell him, Step?' he asked at last. 'What did you say, *exactly*?'

'Say?' Imogen frowned, trying to remember. 'Well, nothing really. I was so—well, you know—so startled, and shocked.

I think I just put the phone down. I might have said "Nonsense!" or "don't be ridiculous!" or something like that. But that's all. Nothing, really.'

'You didn't challenge him, then? Or ask him anything? Like what had put such an idea into his head? If he'd heard it from someone . . . ?'

'No. I told you. I was just—well—thrown, for the moment. I couldn't think *what* to say. I suppose I *should* have said something—made it clear that whatever it is he's trying to do, it's an absolute non-starter, because here I was, at home, two hundred miles away, when—when it all happened. They know I was here—the hospital, I mean—because they phoned me up straight away. I could have told him all that, I suppose.'

'You could, yes. Just the same as you told the police.' Robin drew deeply on his newly-lit cigarette. 'But that wasn't quite what was in the papers, was it? "widow's story queried", I seem to remember: and "the missing hours of grief". That sort of thing. Maybe this Teri creature read them, too? If he *can* read, that is to say—he'd be on the Science side, wouldn't he? All the same, they can count, these science chappies: they're numerate. The "24 hours" bit would have been comprehensible to him. He could even have checked on it, if he'd thought it worthwhile. It looks as if he did, doesn't it? Tell me, Step, what *were* you doing during those twenty-four hours? I've often wondered.'

*

And that makes two of us, thought Imogen wryly. That a woman should carry on for a whole day, telling no one, behaving as if nothing had happened, after receiving news of her husband's death, seemed to her now as incredible as it had seemed to everyone else: and yet, at the time, she had not felt that she was doing anything particularly strange. 'Well, it was Sunday, you see,' she'd explained to the police—as if Sunday was a day that didn't exist, as other days do. They'd seemed to understand, after a while. They were even quite sympathetic, in an embarrassed sort of way; but by then it was too late to alter what she'd said to the newspaper reporters. The lies she'd told them were already rolling off the press.

It was only one lie, really; a small fib told to the young man from the local paper. 'Monday,' she'd told him, 'yes, two o'clock on Monday morning.' The lie seemed, at the time, the easiest way of explaining her peculiar inaction all through Sunday. How could she have guessed that this offhand young reporter, who'd kept glancing at his watch while she talked, was going to bother to check her statement against the police report? Or that the discrepancy he revealed was going to be seized on by other papers—short of news, as it happened, that week— so that eager young men and women would come knocking on her door, notebooks poised, eyes bright, and a good story almost in the bag?

A good story. Ivor would have liked that. As the hero of a good story he had lived, and no doubt would have wished to have died. Which was all very well: but what else could she, his widow, have done, except lie, and go on lying?

5

So hard it is to remember a season gone, a way of life now over. To recall, while the wet white fog coils against the black branches of the winter trees just beyond the window, that only two months ago it had been a golden September day, an Indian summer, and Ivor out there in the sunshine, gathering up dead leaves for the bonfire he would never light. The first bonfire of the season, and he excited as a child about it—a child launching into its fifty-ninth autumn. Excited, too, about tomorrow's lecture, which he had spent half the vacation preparing: the Hanfield Memorial Lecture, to be delivered two hundred miles away, to an audience of over a thousand learned colleagues from all over the world. It was a singular honour, this Hanfield Memorial Lecture, the culmination of a brilliant career. It was a prize, and Ivor had won it, as he had won so many prizes. Imogen, watching from the kitchen window, had seen the easy swing of his arms as he gathered up the leaves, the triumphant toss of his tawny hair in the sunshine, and had thought, 'Thank God he's in a good mood'—and had gone upstairs to pack his things. Ivor could be terrible sometimes, when an important lecture was ahead of him; though no one would ever have guessed it. Even

Imogen herself, watching him on the platform, relaxed, witty, utterly professional, holding his audience in the hollow of his hand—even she, herself, could sometimes hardly believe that this was the same man who had been tearing his family's nerves to shreds only an hour or two before.

*

There wasn't much to pack. Just the few things he'd need for a single night at the hotel where he was to stay when the lecture was over. Why he had decided not to stay there, but to set off, a little after midnight, on the two-hundred mile drive along the wet roads, no one would ever know. Well, probably not, anyway. What was the point of knowing? What could anyone have done if they *had* known . . . ?

*

If . . . if . . . if. *If* he had gone up by train, with Professor Ziegfeld. *If* Imogen had reminded him to take his proper driving glasses instead of relying on his bifocals. *If* she had insisted on accompanying him despite his nervous insistence that he needed to be alone. *If* the long spell of glorious weather hadn't broken that very evening in floods of autumnal rain. If . . . if . . . if . . . By now, eight weeks later, Imogen's brain was quite numbed by thinking of all the ways in which it mightn't have happened.

Not at the beginning, though. At the beginning, her brain had seemed unusually alert, and curiously detached. She hadn't even felt surprised to get a long-distance call from the hospital in the middle of the night: it was as if she had been expecting it all along.

'Yes,' she'd said. 'Yes, I see. Yes, thank you very much. Thank you for telling me,' and she'd set down the phone and gone into the kitchen to look at the time.

Three forty-five a.m.: and presently, just as it was getting light, it all happened all over again. The police, this time.

'Thank you. Yes. Thank you,' she said once more and then, 'No, I'm not alone, my son's here,' she'd lied; and heard the relief in the bothered, unknown voice before it pinged into silence.

Ha ha! Foiled! She felt cunning, a bit of a devil, for having brought off the small deception. Now they'd leave her alone, stop pestering her. Stop trying to foist Ivor's death on her like a wrongly-addressed parcel.

He couldn't be dead yet, she wasn't ready for it, he'd have to wait. He'd said he wouldn't be back till the Sunday evening, and now here he was, dead, first thing in the morning. It was too soon, too early, how could she be ready at such an hour? Besides, she was busy, there was too much to do.

Like the jumble.

'Yes, it's just about ready,' she said vaguely, bundling the last oddments into a cardboard box while Mrs Fielding from the Red Cross stood, smiling and tired, in the damp sunshine outside.

'Yes, quite well, thank you,' Imogen heard herself saying, like a parrot, as she edged Mrs Fielding and the cardboard box, and all the bits and pieces, off the premises. 'Yes, fine, thanks . . . Yes, we really must, mustn't we? . . . Yes, one of these days . . . Yes, that would be very nice . . . Yes. Thank you. Yes . . .'

Gone at last. Again Imogen felt this flicker of sly triumph. Because, of course, all the while no one knew what had happened, then it *hadn't* happened. Not quite. Not yet. It was like a game, this dodging about, putting them off the scent, not letting herself get trapped into telling them.

How long could she keep it up?

All day, apparently, while the tap dripped into the sink, and the tin clock ticked noisily, racing perilously onwards, heedless of its destination: until towards dusk, it faltered, and fell silent, because it hadn't been wound.

'Very well, thank you,' she heard her parrot voice saying, quite brightly, to the two or three people who rang up about this or that during the course of the long afternoon, and then during the quietly encroaching night. Yes thank you. Yes, of course. And yes, the lecture had gone off very well, thank you, wasn't that nice?

So it had, probably, very likely, for all she knew: but this time, as she laid the phone down, she felt, for the very first time, a tiny flicker of unease. Something, somewhere, was not quite as it should be.

The feeling passed, though, in less than a second: and she was sitting listening to the tap again, quite peacefully. It was like an old friend by now, restful and undemanding. She could have stayed in its company for ever.

It was a sort of laziness, really, putting-off Ivor's death like this. Like putting-off the writing of a difficult letter. Tomorrow would be time enough.

*

But when tomorrow came, it came with a thundering on the door: with a sobbing, and a clamour, and tumult of questions and answers as they all surged in: and carelessly, through the swinging front door, they let Reality slip in past them. Out of the windy autumn morning, early still, with the clatter of milk-bottles, the thing came at her, like a gigantic wave, and sent her reeling.

'*Dead*!' she gasped, staring at them. 'Ivor *dead?*' and such was her blankness, her total, unfeigned shock, that no one—until a little later, it was forced upon them—would ever have dreamed that she had heard the news already: had known it all perfectly well for more than twenty-four hours.

'Professor's widow pretends husband still living!' proclaimed one of the dailies a couple of mornings later; and really, you could hardly blame them, such a mix-up it all was of conflicting reports.

'I *wasn't* pretending, I was only lying!' Imogen sobbed when she saw it: and 'There, there' said her bewildered relatives, patting and stroking, and assuring her that they quite understood.

They didn't, of course: and neither did Imogen: but quite soon the need for understanding was overlaid by the need to organise cars for the funeral, and to sort out the squabbles about the flowers. Someone who'd sent a huge wreath of lilies had had their name affixed to a meagre bunch of wilting chrysanthemums; and for a while, naturally, this had taken precedence over grief and loss.

*

But how to summarise all this for Robin? There he lay, lounging against the pillows, expectant, only thirty years old, and still thinking that there are explanations for things. He was waiting for his stepmother to tell him the true story in words—and not too many of them, at that. He was curious about the mystery, certainly, but on guard lest it should prove boring.

'I don't know, Robin. That first day—I told you—I can't remember much about it. The doctor said I was in a state of shock—'

As she spoke, she realised, for the first time, that the doctor had been quite simply right. She *had* been in a state of shock. Until now, it had seemed like a guilty excuse.

Excuse for what? Heartlessness? Cowardice? Or simply for depriving Ivor of his first, exciting day of being mourned? He'd have resented that, certainly, and there was no way, now, of restoring it to him. First love, first job, first day of being dead—they only come once, and if you've missed them, you've missed them.

'Does it matter?' she asked after a moment, finding Robin's eyes still fixed on her, thoughtfully.

He shrugged.

'Only to me,' he answered drily. '*You're* in the clear, as you pointed out, because of all those phone calls, proving that you were innocently at home all night. But you see, Step, in the course of the night's phone-in you seem to have mentioned to someone that your son was there with you.

'I wasn't: and that's made them curious, you see, to know where I *was*. And I don't see why I should tell them.'

6

For lunch, she cooked apple pie, with a sprinkling of castor sugar on top, just as in the old days. It was funny to be feeling interested enough to bother with that sort of thing; but of course it was because of Robin being here. He deserved a nice pudding after obligingly working through all that pâté for his first course, and nothing to go with it but sliced bread. There weren't even any tomatoes.

No more had been said about the unfortunate topic of Imogen's first day as a widow, and she was beginning to hope that perhaps Robin was already bored with the subject, even though it concerned himself. The past and its tedious crop of troubles was something he'd always avoided when he could: he was a child of the future, for ever off into next week before yesterday could properly catch up with him. At the moment, he seemed all agog with his plans for moving back home.

'Listen, Step. Your old bedroom—yours and Dad's—here he gasped on a mouthful of hot apple, and had to snatch a cooling gulp of water from his glass—'I was looking around it this morning while you were down here, and I've decided it'll do. It's got everything. Painful memories (so that *you* won't want it), and lots of cupboard space. Those cupboards are just what I need. If we could just get Dad's junk shifted . . . .'

'Your father's manuscripts!' Imogen was shocked. 'All his articles, poems, translations—right back to his schooldays! And a lot of it never published—no other copies in existence! You don't understand, Robin: your father was a distinguished man. His manuscripts will be very valuable, one day.'

'Then let them accrue value elsewhere,' Robin retorted. 'Let them acquire merit in some dark corner of the cellar, like mushrooms. They don't need a nice, big, sunny room like that just for growing valuable in. I need the space.'

'Robin—!' Again Imogen opened her mouth to protest: but what was the use? This subterranean current of hostility and ridicule which had animated Robin's every mention of his father for as long as she could remember, was something that she had fought against vainly for years. Now that Ivor was dead, and beyond its sting, why go on fighting? It had never been the slightest use, even when he'd been alive.

And anyway, there was nothing wrong with Robin's proposal in itself. In fact, it was a very practical one. It *would* be rather nice to have the empty, ghost-ridden room brought to life again: to draw its teeth and blunt its claws by daily, vigorous use. This way, it would no longer be a threat, lying in wait for her at the head of the stairs. No longer would she feel impelled either to avoid it or to wander into it, as she had done this morning: to hang about there, looking round, weighed down by memories and by the thought that, sooner, or later, she would have to do something about it. About the big, useless four-poster bed, for a start—Ivor's folly, and his pride and joy. Where, now that Ivor was gone, would you ever again find folly on such a scale—the

47

spending, on impulse, of eight hundred pounds at a country auction on an object which couldn't even be got up the stairs until a firm of antique-dealers had come and taken it to pieces and reassembled it? And all just because he *wanted* it? Fools of this sort of stature just don't exist any more.

Robin hadn't said anything about the bed. Presumably that meant he liked it—or at least didn't mind it. Maybe four-poster beds were the in-thing nowadays? All the same, he must have forgotten how much his father had loved it, or surely he'd be sneering by now, urging that the thing be put out for the dust-men? Not that the dustmen would have taken it: but it's the thought that counts.

Meantime, the manuscripts. They could go in Dot's old room for the time being. And why not, at the same time, clear Ivor's study a bit—get rid of some of the papers there—make a bit of space . . . ?

Space for what? For whom? At the thought of Ivor's study being used by anyone else, ever, Imogen's mind shied like a bucking horse; then, as the shock subsided, she timidly and with infinite caution edged back to the notion, examining it curiously, from a safe distance.

A divan under the window, with bright cushions. A small, sturdy table, with perhaps a couple of drawers, in place of Ivor's huge, mahogany roll-top desk, still crammed with papers. Some of them, surely, could be thrown away . . . . Holiday brochures . . . old receipts . . . ?

Throwing things out. Moving things around. Apple-pie with castor-sugar sprinkled on it. Imogen was aware of something stirring in the numbed centre of her being. Something was cracking open a little, shifting, like ice at the coming of the Arctic spring.

A desire to move furniture is a desire for life.

'Right!' she said, getting briskly to her feet. 'You shall have your cupboards, Robin. Let's get started, shall we? It'll be good to get *one* room clear, at least. And after that, we must think about the rest of the house. Everyone's been on at me about it being too big, and it *is*. Even with you here as well—and I don't suppose you'll be staying here for ever—it's still much bigger than we need. Five bedrooms—and three perfectly good attics. We must have lodgers, Robin. Students, or something. Some of Dad's old students, perhaps . . . he'd have liked that . . . .'

'You bet he would! Raving it up in his study all night. Standing bottles of Coke on the Bechstein. Using his first-edition Hazlitt to stop the windows rattling. You bet he'd have liked it! And what else, Step? What else would Dad have liked? We ought to decide, oughtn't we, if we're going to organise the house according to his wishes.'

'Robin, don't!' The protest was futile, but it burst from her uncontrollably. 'Why must you be so unkind, always, about Dad? All fathers make mistakes occasionally . . . surely, now you're a grown man, you can understand . . . ?'

'Oh, I understand all right. I've understood perfectly, ever since I was four years old. Three-and-a-half, to be exact—I'll tell you about it one day. But the point is, Step, where has it got me, all this understanding? Tell me that, Step: *Where's it got me?*'

Imogen did not answer. There were moments when she realised that she was not only shocked by Robin's bitterness against

49

his father, she was scared by it. As always, she sheered away, tried to change the subject.

'Come on; let's get started,' she said, for the second time. 'If you could fetch some of those big cardboard boxes, Robin, out of the dining-room—and I'll start emptying the cupboards in . . . in the bedroom . . . . Get an idea of what's really there . . . .'

Robin had been right, actually—as he so often and so unde-servedly was. It *was* junk, an awful lot of it. Many of the yellowing piles of typescript were mere carbons of other yellowing piles: five or six copies, sometimes, and the handwritten original as well—surely one didn't have to keep *all* of them . . . ?

And then there were the journals, hundreds and hundreds of them, going back over thirty years and more, and only a tiny proportion of them actually containing an article by Ivor him-self. You had to be careful, though: sometimes there might be a letter of his among the Correspondence: or an erudite Latin pun, tucked away at the bottom of a page. And quite often, alongside some yellowing, scholarly paragraph, there would be a furious pencilled line, wiggly with long-evaporated rage, and flanked by exclamation marks—two, three, or even four of them, highlighting the ancient blunder whose heinousness no one would ever bother about again.

What was the point of keeping such stuff? How could you dare to throw it away?

Squatting on the floor, harvesting dust under her nails and in the cracks of her hands, Imogen worked and sorted, the piles growing and toppling at her side, while Robin padded in and out, gathering them up, following her directions—but patron-isingly, with a half-smile, as if he was above it all really, just playing with the grown-ups to oblige. Even though it was his cupboards that were being cleared.

It was always like this. Robin's sudden enthusiasms would galvanise his friends into action on his behalf, they would throw themselves into the thing with a will, only to find, half-way, that he had shuffled off on to their shoulders the wanting as well as the working: it was *their* job to be enthusiastic now, not his.

Like a virus, really.

'You're like a virus, Robin,' she complained, when he next came into the room: and he agreed at once.

It had been a mistake, though, to distract him: it only stirred up his already-simmering boredom with the whole project. In silence, she passed up to him another load of papers and watched him carry it out of the room. The great thing was to keep him going, get the task finished before his awful, uncontrollable boredom took over and left you stranded like a whale on the flat wastelands of his languor and unconcern.

'It's no good going on, Dot's room is full to the chandeliers,' he announced presently, yawning and throwing himself into an armchair: and Imogen, hurrying along the passage to prove that this couldn't possibly be the case, was confronted by a small shock.

Dot had never taken her trunks after all! There they still stood, corded and ready, and stuffed as full as they would hold of all the bits and pieces that Dot had claimed were—or might be, or were jolly well going to be—hers.

Damn! Although the contemplation of so many of Ivor's treasures disappearing under Dot's magpie fingers had somewhat dismayed Imogen at the time, the thought, now, of having

51

them all back again was immeasurably worse. The huge Chinese willow-pattern bowl—already its place on the hall table had become a useful—nay, an indispensable—resting-place of handbags, gloves, library books, telephone messages. The Persian rug, too, out of the drawing-room—already Imogen had noticed how much easier the Hoovering was without it. The familiar landmarks of a lifetime—once they are gone, how swiftly is there no room for them.

Staring morosely at these unwelcome relics of Dot's sojourn here, Imogen, after eight weeks of total lethargy, found herself racked by an intolerable impatience.

'She *must* take them away—I can't have all this clutter everywhere!' she grumbled. 'It's nearly December already, and if we're to have the students settled in by next term . . . .'The students—seriously contemplated only a couple of hours ago—had taken a strange grip on her imagination. Already she had the whole house peopled with them, and they were as delightful, uncomplicated a crowd as you could imagine. Two pleasant, open-faced girls with long fair hair sat studying at a big whitewood table in the spare room, the winter sun pouring in on to their bent heads. A dedicated, poverty-stricken music student was staring, awed, at Ivor's treasured Bechstein—he was touching the notes wonderingly, incredulously—as Ivor would have wished him to be wondering and incredulous—and musing on what a wonderful man it must have been who had owned such a wonderful piano. And there was a classics scholar, of course—or maybe two of them—browsing round Ivor's study, gazing at his splendid collection of books—three walls of them, right up to the ceiling—and they, too, would be thinking how lucky they were; would be handling the collection with reverence and love . . . .

'I'd choose the Depressions rather than the Anxiety States if I were you, Step,' Robin was advising her. 'From the point of view of a landlady, Depressions are a good bet because they lie in bed till midday and don't eat breakfast. Whereas Anxiety States want grapefruit—All-bran—the lot. As well as picking at food all night and drinking coffee. And they have Troubles, too: girlfriends, and indigestion, and frantic phone-calls to places like Aberystwyth. It all costs money. And also, Step, as landlady it'll all be your fault—you'll be *in loco parentis*, which is the Latin for Heads-I-Win, Tails-you-lose. The Sociology Department at Leeds did a survey of landladies, and it proved conclusively that . . .'

'Shush, Robin, I'm trying to think. I must ring up Dot and insist that . . . I mean, I *must* get the rooms clear, mustn't I? Once I've done that, then I'll be able to decide exactly what I'm going to do.'

*

Any widow could have told her. Any property-owner, really. You don't *decide* what happens to your vacant rooms these days, you just fight feebly against whatever does: and after a while, if you are sensible, you give in.

For they are stronger than you are. With their luggage, their determination, and the desperateness of their plight, you don't stand a chance.

Thus it was for Imogen. Within a fortnight, Dot was back,

in tears, and with yet more trunks, containing mountains of clothes and the boys' electric train set. Herbert, apparently, was being impossible again, she just couldn't face it, not over Christmas, and with the kids' holidays starting. And besides—she hastened solicitously to add—she'd felt so guilty about going off and leaving Imogen alone in the empty house. She'd found (rather conveniently, in view of Herbert's current impossibleness) that she couldn't bear the idea of her stepmother being lonely over Christmas, and so—well—here she was. Vernon and Timmie too. They'd cheer Imogen up, wouldn't they, bring a bit of life into the place . . . and Imogen, ticking off in her mind beds, rooms, blankets, food, had somewhat half-heartedly agreed.

Actually, Imogen's loneliness seemed to be proving a godsend all round. Scarcely had Dot established herself in her own room—after a lot of fuss about the piles of papers and manuscripts that had been dumped there in her absence, and shrill insistence on them being moved forthwith to the attic lumber-room—than a telegram arrived from Bermuda announcing Cynthia's arrival on Thursday. All love, and her plane would be arriving at Heathrow at a quarter to seven in the morning, please meet. She, too, had found that she couldn't bear the idea of Imogen being alone over Christmas—evidently no one could who had any very compelling motive for escaping from his own festivities at home.

Even Herbert couldn't, when it came to the point. Impossible he might be, and every bit as selfish as his wife claimed, but all the same the thought of Imogen's loneliness seemed to work on him just as it had on the others, like a stick of gelignite. He arrived, small and shame-faced, and as if the Hounds of Hell were after him, on the day before Christmas Eve.

Imogen, of course, tried to be nice about it: he wasn't *her* husband. She greeted him at least civilly, her brain a-whirl with calculations about where to put him if he and Dot were still supposed to be quarrelling; while Dot, a little in the background, looked him up and down with a knowing, I-told-you-so sort of look.

'There's no room, Herbert, you can't stay,' she began smugly. 'Don't say I didn't tell you . . . !'—and when he didn't say she hadn't, her voice rose to a screech:

'I told you not to do this! I told you! Oh, you're impossible . . . !'

Herbert didn't deny it, though he seemed to have no particular plans for doing anything about it. He listened to Dot's tirade gravely; unpacked his things; had his tea; and then, later in the evening, he and Dot had a long, complicated, sotto voce quarrel behind closed doors. What it was about, Imogen never really learned, but the outcome seemed to be that Herbert wasn't to be sent home after all: he was to stay and be impossible here.

First Dot: then the boys: then Cynthia. All of them uninvited: and now Herbert as well. It was the last straw.

Or so Imogen thought. In fact, it turned out to be the last but one.

'This is Piggy,' announced Robin, leading in out of the darkness a tall, heavily-built girl with a huge suitcase, and a heavy, loosely-braided plait of blonde hair falling over one shoulder. 'I'm not sleeping with her,' he added, glancing round as if for applause.

Actually, of course, it only made things more difficult. Now the girl would have to have a room, a bed, of her own. One of the small attics it would have to be, they were the only rooms left. One of them Imogen had already taken over for herself, until such time as she could make up her mind where she really wanted to be; but there was still the adjoining one, though it would need quite a bit of clearing-out before you could put anyone into it. It would be cold, too . . . Imogen was already short of spare blankets, and sick to death of carrying them up and down stairs.

It was all a great nuisance. What did Robin think he was playing at, anyway? He'd explained that the girl had been thrown out of her flat and had nowhere to go—but why was he letting that bother him? If he wasn't sleeping with her, or borrowing money from her (and you could see at a glance that she had none to be borrowed) then what *was* he doing? What was in it for him? Christmas spirit?

It was eerie. Really it was.

7

Christmas in the House of Mourning: Edith, with many meaning looks, sympathy firing on all cylinders, brought in a pot of white hyacinths, but only because there were no such things as black ones. Imogen thanked her nervously, and waited to see from which direction the next assault would be launched. 'A Quiet Christmas' everyone had earnestly agreed— and you could see them, as they spoke, working out just how much it would save, and what they could do with the money. No presents, it wouldn't seem right, Yippee! And now, after all that, here they were, one after the other, twitching packages guiltily from behind their backs and shoving them at her as if they were dirty postcards. Soap. Bath salts. Writing-paper. All the things that a widow might reasonably be expected still to have some use for. And because they'd promised not to give her anything, and were breaking the promise, she had to be extra grateful and thank them twice, once for the present and once for the betrayal.

But one of the betrayals—Cynthia's—was a magnificent one: a brilliantly expensive Kaftan, covered in gold embroidery, and glitteringly unsuitable for anything except the kind of parties that Imogen would never be going to again. It would have been all right for the kind of parties she sometimes used to go to with Ivor; and he would have liked her to wear a thing like this. Would have liked it, that is, all the while she remained at his side, manifestly his possession; but on the other hand, he hated her to remain at his side at parties: it cramped his style with the beautiful wives of important husbands. And so actually it would all have been rather complicated. Her grief for Ivor was always running into tangles like this: no sooner did she get thinking, Oh, how Ivor would have loved this, than she had a sudden vision of how it would actually have been.

And somehow the truth made her feel like crying even more. Funny.

Still, you don't cry on Christmas morning. Not with everyone looking at you and wondering if you are going to, and what they are supposed to do about it if you do.

'Oh, *thank* you, Cynthia, how lovely!' she enthused, shaking out the glittering folds and holding it up for inspection. 'Look, Dot! Look, all of you! Isn't it gorgeous?'

'Beautiful,' said Dot, disapproving. It wasn't that she was shocked, exactly, or disliked the garment in itself: it was just that she could see at a glance that no good would come of it. Some women have this gift.

Herbert's eyes were almost popping out of his head.

'It's the tops!' he cried. 'You'll be quite the cat's whiskers!'— two expressions which—as he must surely have known—his wife couldn't endure. To have a husband who is impossible, that's one thing, and you can complain about it to your friends without loss of status: but to have a husband who is *vulgar* . . .

'*Herbert!*' was all she said, and he subsided at once, while Imogen, still murmuring her embarrassed gratitude, re-folded the glittering thing and laid it back in its tissue-paper under Cynthia's self-satisfied scrutiny. You could see that Cynthia had won: but without, as yet, having any idea what the battle was about.

It was about Ivor, of course—what else? Even dead, she couldn't leave him alone.

During the five days since Cynthia's arrival at Heathrow, nearly four hours late and having mislaid her vaccination certificate, Imogen had almost forgotten about her visitor having once been Ivor's wife. She seemed more like an Act of God, scattering scarves, luggage, presents, hairspray all over the house and wanting to sleep with her head to the north, and with three hot-water-bottles. She couldn't eat parsnips, or anything fried, and every mealtime started with her crying out 'Where are my pills?' Three lots of them there were—white ones for her nerves, yellow ones for her blood-pressure, and pink ones for—what was it?—migraine, or something. They'd been prescribed by her doctor in Bermuda, a dear, lovely man. *Promise* me, he'd said to Cynthia, *promise* me you'll take them regularly while you're in England; and she'd promised. If only—Imogen mused darkly—if only the dear, lovely doctor could have made her promise also to put them back in the same place at the end of each meal. But alas, he hadn't. Handbags, pockets, drawers had to be ransacked day after day, while the food cooled on the table, and everyone felt they must stop eating so as to look as if they were helping, and Cynthia clambered back and forth past their chairs, joggling the table, and saying she didn't want to be a nuisance.

*

And now here she was waiting for Imogen to say something. Stick her neck out—put her foot in it—something. That gleaming, over-generous present had been a lead-in.

Imogen waited.

Forgiveness. That's what it was. Cynthia forgave her; wanted bygones to be bygones. Christmas, surely, was the time for burying the hatchet?

Indeed yes. But what hatchet? Which bygones? Imogen didn't want to be behindhand in Christmas charity, but she couldn't make out what it was all about. It wasn't as if Ivor had left Cynthia for Imogen; he'd left her for peace and quiet, and freedom, and punctual well-cooked meals. Imogen couldn't see how forgiveness came into it, in either direction, especially after all this time.

But this, for some reason, simply made Cynthia burst into tears, and declare that Imogen didn't understand, had never understood: which of course was true. But where do you go from there?

'I know you despise me,' Cynthia sobbed, 'you always have! You think I'm just stupid and impractical and silly . . . maybe I am, but all the same, Ivor loved me, he'd have wanted me to have my rights . . . he loved me just the way I am! He'd had enough of clever women, his first wife was a right blue-stocking, and years and years older than him . . . if you'd ever met her, you wouldn't wonder that he ended up falling for a silly, feather-brained, harum-scarum little thing like me . . . .'

No? Imogen reflected on this whole harum-scarum little

trip all the way from Bermuda just in time for the dividing-up of Ivor's estate: she pondered, too, on the feather-brained little phone-calls to solicitors and lawyers that had been going on . . . and suddenly her eyes filled with tears. Ivor, why aren't you laughing? Can't you hear my wicked, uncharitable thoughts, off wherever you are?

Naturally, Cynthia thought that the tears in Imogen's eyes were tears of remorse, and at once she was all kindness and sympathy:

'Oh, Imogen, darling, I didn't mean . . . *Of course* I don't hold it against you, my poor dear. Not now, not any longer. That's what I've been trying to tell you, the bitterness is all gone now, it's all been wiped away by this terrible, terrible tragedy. We are sisters in sorrow now, Imogen. Sisters, as Ivor would have wished . . . .'

Ivor would have hated sisters, if he'd had any. He'd have hated the demands they were entitled to make, and the things they could remember about you when you were ten. Shrinking within Cynthia's scented Orlon embrace, Imogen wondered how soon she could decently detach herself, and move out of range. The awful thing was that Cynthia *was* being kind, in a way. Just as Edith was kind, and Dot, and Herbert. In their separate ways, and with due regard to their own interests, they were all being kind.

But what can friends do for you when what you really need is enemies? People on whom to try out your precarious, convalescent aggression: people you can fight with, score off, not bother about. Sorry, didn't mean to hit you, just wanted to find out if I still could . . . .

*

Roast turkey. They'd promised there wouldn't be, but there was. Robin brought Piggy down to join the family meal, her plait tied with a shoe-lace, but she'd taken one look and gone off to cook herself some Macrobiotic rice. Which of course made everyone feel more guilty than ever.

'For the children . . .' they said, helping themselves to sprouts, bread-sauce, gravy. 'Christmas is for the children . . .' A heavy burden, you'd have thought, for two such small boys, one of whom didn't like stuffing.

After dinner there were more presents—'for the children', of course: two fragile, ecstatic little props on which the whole vast, dark day was balanced, more precariously than they could ever know.

No tree. The anxious, behind-doors debate on this issue had been mercifully resolved only yesterday by the discovery that the trees were all sold out. And so now the boys' presents lay in a heap on the carpet, waiting for some sort of uneasy ritual to be improvised. And to complicate matters even further, a legend seemed to be right now in the making that Ivor had been in the habit of dressing up as Father Christmas and hand-ing out presents to his grandsons with beaming bonhomie and idiotic chatter about reindeer and chimneys and the rest. Imo-gen was aware of an anxious, whispered conference going on in the corner of the room as to whether Herbert should, or should not, take over this rôle—or non-rôle, rather, for none of it, to Imogen's recollection, had ever happened. Mercifully, the debate ended in a decision that he shouldn't; and with whoops of happy greed, the boys fell on their parcels without ceremony, tearing into the coloured wrappings and lovingly-penned messages like termites into timber. This year, of course, there was no present from Grandpa, but never mind, there were plenty of others.

*

Ivor as Father Christmas! Oh well. In a way, he'd have rather enjoyed the rôle—would certainly have undertaken it if someone from the BBC had asked him to, and had come along with a camera-team to record it—'Professor Barnicott, author of this and this and this, relaxing with his grandsons'—that sort of thing: but it so happened that no one had.

Well, and so why not let him have the legend, then?—this legend that Dot and all of them were so busy concocting? The jovial, benign grandpa, each year bringing the magic of Christmas to his little grandsons? He'd have loved it—of course he would: and all for free, now that he was dead. No boredom. No bother. No risk of the kids wrecking the whole image by crying and squabbling. It was a soft option, being dead. Good old Ivor!

*

Father Christmas, though. And after barely three months. What else would they have done to him, between them, by the time another year had passed—and all the years to follow?

Ivor, Ivor, she cried silently, what are they doing to you?

Come back, just for one moment, and let me look at you, remind myself what you were really like . . . !

But already he was slipping away into the past, smaller and smaller, further and further away, scarlet hood, white beard and all.

*

'Granny! I say, Granny!'

Imogen roused herself, with an effort. There at her side was Timmie, gazing up into her face wide-eyed, and slightly aggrieved. 'Granny, I thought Grandpa was supposed to be dead? Well, he isn't. He's still here. In his study, all dressed up as Father Christmas! Why isn't he dead, Granny, like he's meant to be?'

8

Naturally, nobody told Timmie off for telling lies. For one thing, it was Christmas, and for another, as Dot pointed out, there are no such things as lies nowadays, there is only the inability to distinguish between fantasy and reality. On top of which, Timmie, it seemed, took after her, he was very sensitive really, and this was his way of coming to terms with his grief.

If any. To be honest, he and his grandfather had never really hit it off. Timmie was inclined to spoil Ivor's most impressive reminiscences by saying things like 'Who's Churchill?' Still, he must feel *something* about his grandfather's death; it was a relief, in a way, to see some sign of it at least.

And so, after the first stunned moments, Timmie was treated as a cross between an invalid and an O.B.E., everyone vying with one another to respect his feelings and hoping that someone else would ask the insensitive questions which would get him talking.

Because it *was* rather mysterious. There had, of course, been a mass surge towards the study right at the beginning, and an uneasy, half-embarrassed search had been undertaken, but naturally nothing was to be found. No Father Christmas costume. Nothing.

'What makes you so sure it was Grandpa?' someone ventured to ask him. 'I mean, anyone could dress up as Father Christmas . . . ?'

Timmie seemed, for a moment, to be puzzled by the question.

'He was in his big chair, that no one else may sit in,' he began. 'He had his glasses on, and he was reading one of his big books—the Greek book, the very big one. And he was cross,' Timmie added, as if this clinched the identification. 'He jumped up and sort of came at me, like I'd done something awful. And I *hadn't*, Mummy, I hadn't touched a thing. And I never meant to interrupt him. I mean, he's supposed to be dead. It's not *fair*!'

Of all this array of evidence, nothing remained for public scrutiny except the Greek Lexicon. There it lay, the large Liddell and Scott, open, and balanced on the arm of Ivor's big leather chair, just as it always used to be when he was working. But of course that didn't prove anything, anyone could have put it there. No one had, but obviously they could have. No point in making a drama of it, anyway.

The questions and arguments teetered this way and that. Someone must have been looking up a word for a crossword puzzle? What, in *Greek*? Well, just looking up a word, then. But none of us *knows* any Greek . . . .

Suddenly, Imogen could bear no more of it. She slammed the big Lexicon shut, and leaned across the armchair to put it away on the low shelf where it belonged. And now, with the only piece of tangible evidence thus removed, the whole puzzle seemed suddenly to disintegrate. There was nothing more to be explained, no more to be said. Timmie was reassured that it couldn't possibly have been Grandpa—not that he seemed to be all that bothered—and the subject was dropped, except for Dot saying 'I told you so!'

She hadn't, of course, how could she? But it turned out that she wasn't referring specifically to Timmie's recent implausible recital, but to an earlier, and more generalised prediction of hers to the effect that whatever Herbert did, he always managed to make a mess of it. Apparently not dressing up as Father Christmas came into this category; he couldn't even not do *that* without making a mess of it.

Well, this seemed to be the gist of it, anyway, as far as Imogen could make out through the open door. Most of the time, she tried to keep out of the way when Herbert and Dot were quarrelling, but it was difficult when they quarrelled on the stairs: which they often did, because it was commonly Herbert's attempt to escape unobtrusively up to their room that jogged Dot's memory about whatever it was that he had or hadn't done.

And that, to all intents and purposes, was the end of the episode. For some reason, Imogen could not bring herself to tell the rest of them about the small additional shock she had received while they weren't noticing. Leaning over to put the Lexicon back on the shelf, she had caught a whiff of whisky: and on investigating more closely, she discovered a whisky bottle and a recently-used glass standing exactly where Ivor used to stand them—on the floor between the armchair and the bookshelves.

Someone had been sitting in Ivor's chair this afternoon, drinking whisky and reading Greek, just as he used to drink and read. Downing glass after glass, perhaps, as he had been wont to do while he waited for the bloody visitors to go . . . . For a moment, leaning heavily over the chair arm, Imogen could have sworn she smelt traces of his pipe as well, and heard him clearing his throat: but that, of course, was fantasy.

Who had it been, sitting here? Obviously, she could have questioned them all, but somehow she knew already that they were all going to say No, and what would be the point of that?

Why look for trouble—Easier by far just to wash up the glass, throw away the empty bottle, and then the whole mystery would cease to exist. Just as the mystery of the Lexicon had ceased to exist the moment she had put it back on the shelf where it belonged. How safe it looked, how settled, big and shabby and solid, next to the Classical Dictionary, just where it had always been.

*

It was nearly a week later when the next peculiar thing happened. 'You must have got a poltergeist here, darling,' Cynthia had said, half-laughing, half-scared. But then, Cynthia was by nature given to exaggeration. In actual fact, the whole thing *might* have been just some silly kind of a muddle. With all these ill-assorted people in the house, brought together by nothing more unifying than a need to get away from somewhere else, there were bound to be misunderstandings.

Once again, it was Timmie who had first stumbled upon the thing, but this time his brother Vernon had been with him. It had been a grey, not-quite-freezing afternoon just before the

New Year, and the first Imogen knew of anything being amiss was the sound of shrill, childish voices, furiously protesting, just beneath her window. Then a deeper voice—a man's voice— interrupting, overriding easily the high, indignant chirping.

For a while, Imogen paid no attention. Lying idly on her bed, half-reading, half-day-dreaming, she felt a vast reluctance to bestir herself. Although it was barely three o'clock, the winter afternoon was already on the wane. For some time now, she had been notic- ing the shadows gathering in the angles of the ceiling. The sharp rectangle of light from the dormer window was a silvery purple now instead of white; soon it would be too dark to read.

It was the front attic that was 'her' room for the time being—the smallest of the three attics that spanned the width of the house under the roof. The adjoining one was Piggy's; and the third, and largest, was still a lumber-room, as it had been for years.

This attic was Imogen's room only temporarily, of course. When all this turmoil of comings and goings had subsided (Imogen was still enough of a novice at widowhood to believe that it might), then she would choose one of the rooms down on the first floor for her own. *Really* her own, furnished according to her own taste, and not to the taste of Ivor's ghost. She would buy cheap, bright rugs that hadn't come from Persia or Benares or anywhere. She would fill the shelves with paperback novels and pots of trailing ivy, and hang on the walls pictures which hadn't been presented by the artist in grateful recognition of this, that or the other.

Her pictures, not Ivor's. It was high time Ivor got moving. It wasn't fair to be dead and yet to stay around like this, in every room, in every corner of the house . . . . There ought to be something like a fly-spray, a fly-spray for ghosts, a ghost-spray . . . .

Ivor would have laughed at that, if he'd been in one of his good moods. No, he wouldn't, he'd have called it whimsy, with that impatient twist of the mouth that he kept for fools . . . .

*

Oh, shut up, you're dead, who cares what *you* think? You have no business telling me what's whimsy and what isn't, not any longer.

Get out! Get out! Get out!

*

The dispute outside seemed to be escalating. In one of the childish voices she could hear the beginning of tears.

But still she lay there, doing absolutely nothing. Hell, they were Dot's children, let *her* sort it out. And Robin—yes, that male voice now rising beyond irritation and into anger was certainly his—Robin was Dot's brother, not Imogen's. Nothing to do with Imogen really, none of them. No blood-tie at all. At intervals over the years, whenever Ivor's family life became more than she could cope with, she had attempted to console herself with these sort of reflections, but it never worked for long. Blood may be thicker than water, but when it comes to family quarrels, it's being *there* that puts you in the wrong. It is one's presence, not one's genes, that lands one with all the responsibility.

And that was why she was lying so very quietly right now. Let her so much as put her head out of the window into the biting December dusk, and call out 'What's going on?' and she would at once be to blame for the whole thing, and responsible for putting it right. She would be called upon to decide whether something was *fair* or not; whether Dot was or wasn't spoiling her brats rotten . . . .

*

It was unusual, though, to hear Robin yelling at the kids like this. He didn't like children, admittedly, and of course children are very intuitive about this sort of thing, and gather round the child-hater like flies round a honey-pot. Luckily, as well as disliking them, Robin was also very good at not noticing they existed, and so normally there was very little trouble, except when Dot caused it by complaining to her brother that he treated the children as *things*, not *people*.

But they *were* things, Robin would retort, wide-eyed: to think of children as people was sheer anthropomorphism— and a brother-and-sister slanging-match would ensue, to which the boys would listen with the greatest of interest. What sort of complexes it was giving them was hard to tell. They were happy children, and correspondingly difficult to fathom.

They didn't sound very happy at the moment, though. Not Vernon, anyway.

'We didn't!' he was shrieking. 'We didn't, we didn't, we didn't . . . !'

'And if you say we're liars'—Timmie took up the grievance

even more shrilly—'If you say we're liars, then you're just a . . .'

But before he had selected from his fairly extensive vocabulary exactly the word that would best describe his uncle, a sharp crunching on the gravel told Imogen that Robin was getting out.

Worsted? Triumphant? Bored with the whole thing? Robin was the only man Imogen had ever known who could even be bored by victory.

*

It would have been easier to discover what it had all been about if they hadn't all told her at once, each with an escalating conviction of the justice of his cause that made the crockery on the tea-table ring. It would have been easier, too, if Dot hadn't been arguing, in top register, from two somewhat contradictory premises: first, that her sons hadn't touched a thing and had never been anywhere near Uncle Robin's room: and second that none of this would have happened if Herbert had taken them out for a Sunday afternoon walk, like other fathers.

The four-poster bed. This, Imogen quickly gathered, was the storm-centre of the dispute. The four-poster bed in the room which had once been hers and Ivor's, and was now Robin's. Someone (and here the voices rose to such a pitch of assertion and denial that Piggy, who was apparently unused to family life, murmured 'Oh no . . . !' and hurried from the room)— *someone* had dragged all those old papers down from the attic again and dumped them all over the bed! Not to mention pulling the pillows about, messing around with the curtains, and generally leaving the place looking like a battle-field.

'Well, *of course* it was the bloody kids: who else could it be?' Robin demanded.

A good question. But all the same, Dot remained unshaken in her conviction that her sons would never dream of . . . well, of whatever it was; how could she be expected to make head or tail of it with everyone going on at her like this?

Playing *houses*? Fighting with *pillows*? Impossible! And anyway, all normal children play this sort of game, it's ridiculous to make such a fuss about it. Besides, no one had ever told them *not* to play in that room. Why, not so long ago it had been the room belonging to their dear grandfather . . . .

The implied suggestion that in his lifetime Ivor would have smilingly allowed the boys to romp on his precious bed and throw his manuscripts about, reduced everyone momentarily to stunned silence; and when, one by one, they took up the threads of the dispute again, it was in an altogether quieter and more coherent manner, so that Imogen was at last able to piece together some sort of a picture of what must have actually happened. It must have been something like this.

Sunday afternoon. The grown-ups all asleep, or sunk in impenetrable lethargy. Boredom stalked the place, hounding the little boys from room to room, up and down the staircases, until presently it brought them to the threshold of the room which had once been Granny's and Grandpa's. Some impulse (grief, claimed Dot, when she wasn't claiming that it hadn't happened at all) made them open the door and peep in.

To their surprise, the curtains round the bed were closely

drawn. They had never seen it like this before—indeed, until that moment they hadn't realised that the bed *had* curtains. Intrigued, and a little scared, they had tiptoed nearer; parted the curtains an inch or two; whereupon—

'We saw a wizard!' shrilled Timmie. 'He was sitting in the middle of the bed casting spells . . . !'

Spells? What do you mean, spells?

'*Spells. You* know. Magic. He was all hunched up and muttering magic words!'

'No, he wasn't'—Vernon corrected his small brother—'He was only—'

'Yes, he was . . .'

'No, he wasn't . . .'

Darlings, darlings. Don't shout so. One at a time. *Who* was . . . ? Why do you say it was a wizard . . . !

'Because it *was* a wizard . . . !'

'He was certainly wearing a wizard's hat,' confirmed Vernon judicially, 'I suppose he might have just put it on for fun, but he did look very wizard-y. And he was writing funny signs . . .'

'Magic signs, all triangles and things'—Timmie filled in the picture gleefully—'just like the wizard in Ali the Donkey . . . .'

*

And so the story escalated, the adults chipping in here and there as best they might with deflating questions of fact. Well, but what did he *look* like? Old or young?

This drew a blank, because of course wizards aren't old or young, are they, they are just wizards.

Well, was his hair grey? Or what colour?

'Grey,' said Timmie at once; and, 'Black,' simultaneously asserted Vernon.

'Silly, it was his *hat* that was black . . . .'

'No, it wasn't . . . .'

'Yes, it was, and anyway, you couldn't have seen, you were behind me . . . .'

'No, I wasn't . . . .'

'Yes, you were . . . . Besides, wizards always have grey hair . . . .'

'No, they don't . . . .'

'Yes, they do. In Ali the Donkey . . .'

Hush, darlings, hush, not so much shouting! Tell us what happened next? What did he do when he saw you? Well, he didn't see us, not actually; we sort of tiptoed away . . . . Well, why didn't you come straight and *tell* someone . . . ?

'We *did*, Granny! We were just looking for Mummy when Uncle Robin . . .'

*

'It's all lies!'

Robin's voice cut across the discussion with sudden vehemence, and everyone looked up, startled.

'It's all lies. They've made up the whole thing from start to finish. First they wreck my room, and then they try to lie their way out of it. Bloody little vandals! They'll both end up in Borstal . . . .'

Here, Timmie burst diplomatically into tears, and Dot

turned on her brother like a tigress, accusing him of being a bully, a hypocrite, and a sadist.

This cheered him up at once, and he listened with interest to the rest of her accusations. He had done a terrible thing, she told him, the worst thing you can possibly do to a child: he had been *unjust*.

'They'll never trust you again,' she concluded tearfully, 'Never!'

'Oh, rubbish. They never have trusted me. I'm their Wicked Uncle, aren't I, kids?'

The shrieks of delighted assent which this evoked made Dot wince. And later, after tea, she stood watching while her brother settled down to his crossword puzzle with a nephew leaning rapturously over each arm of his chair.

'Why did the fly fly, Uncle Robin?'

'Uncle Robin, have you ever heard of a cat that lived to be thirty-one?'

He didn't answer, he never did, but they didn't seem to mind at all.

'. . . Because the spider spied 'er, Uncle Robin!' they shrieked, in an ecstasy of one-way rapport. 'Uncle Robin, it says in the *Guinness Book of Records* . . .'

*

Dot looked on sourly. She was wondering, as she had wondered all her life long, why it was that love could be earned so easily. In almost any way, it seemed, except by deserving it.

Imogen, too, was watching the little tableau.

He knows something, she was thinking; he knows something that he's not telling us. He may not know who the 'wizard' was, or what he was doing; but he knows *something*.

9

Imogen had decided some while back that on the first of January she was going to feel better. 'My husband died last year', she would be able to say, distancing the thing at a single glorious stroke.

And so when she woke up on the appointed day feeling just as miserable as she had ever felt, the disappointment was almost worse than the grief. She turned and buried her face in the pillow, hiding away from the light of the New Year.

A bright, pure light it was through the small square window of her attic room. White, as if in the night snow had fallen. It hadn't, Imogen knew, because the air didn't feel right; but that's what it looked like when she'd first opened her eyes.

*

Ivor had loved the snow. He loved to quote tags of poetry about it—from Virgil, from Hesiod, from Tennyson—standing at the dining-room window with everyone listening to him. He loved, too, the vast impact he could make on it with such minimal effort, stamping with mighty footsteps up and down to the snow-bound garage; across the flawless whiteness of the lawn and back again. Huge his footsteps looked, as if the Abominable Snowman had been there, having his will of the pure expanse.

'A tramp in the snow . . . .' 'I'm off for a tramp in the snow . . . .' Ivor had loved phrases like these, rolling them round his tongue as he watched from the window, sometimes venturing outside and sometimes not, while the white light filled the house, and Imogen built the fires high.

A tramp in the snow. She could see him now, through her tightly-closed eyes, striding down a white mountain side, very small and far away, and thank goodness not in the Father Christmas outfit. Just his old anorak and boots, and moving *towards* her for once, getting bigger and bigger as she watched. She could see his face now, glowing with the sharp cold, and with the joy of being the one who was out in it, the one who would be able to talk about it all evening to those who had stayed huddled by the fire. She remembered how cold his cheeks would be when she kissed him, chill and exciting from the great outside. And while she made hot coffee, and fussed, as he loved her to do, over his damp socks, he'd be telling her how deep it had been. Three feet . . . four feet. By tomorrow, it would have been five.

She ached for his lies and boasting, and it was like aching for the sun.

*

Four months. Four months gone. It was like a pregnancy; at three months you can expect it to be like this, at four months

79

like that: at five months you will feel it quicken, the new life stirring within you.

But it wasn't happening, she wasn't getting anywhere, nothing inside her was growing. The pain was as bad this morning as it had been on the very first day. No, the second.

I'll never get over it. Never.

*

'You'll never get over it, of course, dear,' was Edith's New Year greeting across the hedge a couple of hours later: and in that moment, suddenly, Imogen knew that she *would* get over it. Knew, with a blind fury of conviction, that one day she would be happy again, would enjoy herself again. Would wake up happy in the morning: would fall asleep looking forward to the new day.

The knowledge was too new, too sudden, to tell to anyone. It must remain a secret as yet: a secret that she hugged to herself, saying not a word. It enabled her to listen to Edith's good wishes as calmly as one might listen to burglars ransacking a building from which all the valuables have already been taken.

'Not a *happy* New Year, Imogen, because we both know that cannot be,' Edith was saying, her lined, indoor face haggard and hungry-looking in the silvery winter sunshine. 'Not a *happy*, but a *peaceful* year, that's what I shall wish for you, my dear: I pray that you may discover what I discovered: that even though happiness is at an end, you may still win through to a kind of peace . . . .'

I won't. If they try to palm me off with peace, I'll throw it at them. Happiness is where I'm going, and I shan't stop till I get there. If Peace comes and gets in the way, I shall kick it.

'Thank you, Edith, and the same to you,' was what she said aloud: and five minutes later, found herself wondering whether Peace hadn't, after all, something to be said for it.

Dot and Herbert were quarrelling again. In the kitchen, this time, which was going to make lunch very, very late. Because, of course, you can't just walk in and start clattering saucepans and washing greens. The quarrels of married couples are sacred; it would be like cooking in church.

Not that you could help hearing what they were saying, whether you went into the kitchen or not. What Dot was saying, anyhow; Herbert, as usual, was keeping pretty quiet, treading the precarious path between saying the wrong thing and not answering when he was spoken to.

It was about That Woman again. The one who was forty if she was a day, who was only out for what she could get, and who didn't know what Love meant. Her hair was dyed, too, in case Herbert hadn't noticed: just take a look at the roots some time.

I don't know what Love means either, Herbert was defending himself, that's what is so restful about her. Here, something hurtled across the kitchen and smashed against the wall. Something cheap, it would be, and easily replaceable—Dot was a prudent sort of a person. She'd have been careful, too, that it didn't actually hit Herbert, perhaps drawing blood, and thus putting him hopelessly in the right about everything for weeks to come.

Even being *missed* by a teacup, though, confers a certain moral ascendancy. Imogen could hear the new confidence in

Herbert's voice as the clatter of broken china died away. Unfortunately, he used his momentary advantage, as men will, for the assembling of facts to support his case. No, the letter he'd slipped into his pocket this morning wasn't from Her, it was from the Inland Revenue—here, see for yourself. No, he hadn't taken Her out to lunch that day, he went back to collect his extra shirts. And no, that wasn't Her on the phone last night at midnight. And anyway, it wasn't midnight, it was only 11.45.

Imogen could only sigh for him. Why is it that men, who so pride themselves on their rational, factual approach, never examine rationally one of the facts about facts: namely, *has* a jealous wife ever actually been pacified by one?

Half past twelve. In about ten minutes, by Imogen's calculations, Dot would start crying; and for approximately fifteen minutes after that Herbert would be apologising, and saying Yes, of course he loved her, he hadn't meant that at all . . . . And then Dot would cry some more—perhaps five minutes—and Herbert would agree (with just the tiniest hint of boredom in his voice by now) that yes, he was a sadist and a monster and a heartless brute . . . .

*

A soft step behind her made Imogen spin round guiltily, caught in the act, caught standing in her own hallway. She had been a landlady (to all intents and purposes) for only a couple of weeks, but it is amazing how quickly a landlady learns to feel like a burglar in her own house, with no right to be anywhere.

But it was only Piggy. Appearing from nowhere as usual,

barefoot, and wearing a draggly floor-length brocade skirt with tassels. She gave Imogen her usual sidelong, evasively disapproving glance, and continued on her unregarding way into the kitchen, right into the firing-line, armoured in a kind of bullet-proof self-absorption that filled Imogen with awe and incredulity. She heard the click and clatter of Piggy's special non-stick saucepan, and the rustle of her Natural Foods in their neat white packets—all of them, actually, looking like packets of bicarbonate of soda. She heard the rattle of the dresser drawer as Piggy searched for her special wooden spoon: and then the tip-tap of natural wood on natural non-stick metal as Piggy stirred her de-hydrated wheat-germ, or whatever. Imogen envied passionately the girl's nerve. If it *was* nerve? Even if it wasn't, even if it was just blank, self-absorbed insensitivity, she still envied it. Had she herself possessed this quality—whatever it was—then the potatoes would have been nearly cooked by now, and lunch on the verge of ready.

From where she stood, beyond the door, Imogen had heard Dot's scandalised little intake of breath at Piggy's intrusion. 'Will you *please* get out of my kitchen,' she'd wanted to say; but of course 'My stepmother's kitchen' doesn't have quite the same ring about it, so she had controlled the impulse, and contented herself with dropping her voice to a strangled mutter; while Herbert stared at the ceiling, humming a little tune, and at intervals saying Well, I suppose. Both of them, it seemed to Imogen, were playing for time, trying desperately not to lose the thread of their quarrel: to keep it, somehow, in a state of suspended animation until Piggy should be gone. It was a desperate business, like trying to keep a goldfish alive while someone rushes to fetch water. Even Imogen, out of sight of the whole thing, could feel the suspense of it.

Not so Piggy. Three minutes, it said, on her packet of powdered compost-grown whatever, and three minutes she gave it, stirring slowly and meditatively, tap-tap-tap, with her wooden spoon, while above and around her, filling the air with its tension, the quarrel hung between life and death, with Herbert and Dot, like surgeon and anaesthetist, locked in a desperate co-operation to keep the thing going.

But it was too late. By the time Piggy left the kitchen, carrying her tray of food and her mug with Please Do Not Bend inscribed on it, the quarrel had already drawn its last, feeble breath. The death-agony was over, and first Herbert, then Dot, left the kitchen, heads bent.

Now, at last, for the potatoes. Hurrying to the sink, Imogen set to work, pausing only to put under the tap the saucepan in which Piggy had scorched her mysterious repast, and to replace the white, medicinal-looking packages on to their shelves. It was a nuisance in a way having Piggy do her own separate meals like this, but the girl seemed to prefer it, and anyway it was difficult to see how her peculiar concoctions could have been fitted in with the family meal.

'I want vitamin-enriched heather-grown mountain honey,' Vernon and Timmie would have been screeching in next to no time: and, 'Not with *parsnips*, dears,' Dot would have countered, scandalised. 'But *she's* having it on her parsnips, Mummy' . . . and so it would have gone on, and on, and on. Better leave well alone.

At first, Imogen had worried a little about Piggy's aloofness and her strange, solitary ways. 'Boyfriend trouble,' Robin had airily explained, but Imogen didn't believe it. Imogen had known a lot of girls in the throes of boyfriend trouble, and in her experience they didn't behave like this at all. On the contrary, they were greatly in evidence most of the time. They hung around, red-eyed, waiting for someone to ask them what was wrong: they hovered over the telephone, ate chocolate cake, and had their girlfriends round for all-night condolence sessions, the earnest voices twittering low and soft behind closed doors as the sufferers lounged against cushions in orange or purple lamplight, assuring one another that he was frightened by the strength of his own feelings: that he didn't trust himself to speak on the phone: that he had phoned twice today already, once while she was in the bath and once while she was out posting the letter. Anything—anything at all—rather than touch on the possibility that he just didn't care all that much, and never had.

Still, Piggy might be different, and present different symptoms. Several times, at the beginning, Imogen had tried to draw her into the family circle, inviting her to join them for meals, and in the sitting-room, and asking her friendly questions about herself. But without being exactly rude, Piggy had an uncomfortable knack of making every approach seem an interference, every question an impertinence. From her laconic replies, they'd so far managed to learn that Yes, she was a student: and No, she wasn't in her first year, she was in her second, sort of. And Yes, she'd known Ivor, sort of, everyone did, but she herself was English, not Classics. No, she didn't usually go home for the vacations: and No, her parents didn't mind, why should they?

This last had brought a little squeal of protest from Cynthia, who, while not a parent herself, was a great believer in people minding things.

'What a hard, disagreeable sort of a girl,' she'd protested to Imogen later on. 'I can't think *why* you let her stay, darling, I really can't. Those awful, shapeless skirts of hers . . . and no shoes . . . and that dreadful dusty black thing she wears, a nun's habit, or something . . . .'

'A burnous,' Imogen explained. 'An Eastern burnous—they were all the rage with the students a year or so back, they used to pay the earth for them second-hand. It's all part of the anti-materialism thing, the anti-establishment—'

But two six-syllable words in succession were too much for Cynthia. She looked pained, wrinkled her nose, and then went on with her own disquisition as if there had been no interruption:

'I mean, Imogen, apart from anything else, it's the sheer cheek of it that gets me. The way she just simply arrived, the day before Christmas, and then just stayed and stayed . . . .'

Look who's talking, Imogen could have said, but didn't; and anyway, Cynthia gave her no chance.

'I don't suppose the wretched girl is even *paying* you anything,' she continued indignantly, swelling with the righteous wrath to which, in a way, she was entitled, having herself insisted on paying for her keep right from the beginning. At first, Imogen had been pleased at the sight of all those voluntarily-proffered pound notes each week—Cynthia was as lavish with money as she was with advice, tears, complaints, and everything else—but quite soon it began to dawn on

Imogen that with these same pound notes Cynthia had quietly bought the right never to go away at all. Ever.

'Piggy *is* paying me, actually,' she now explained—just as if the thing was any of Cynthia's business. 'She's more practical than you'd imagine. She phoned the Student Accommodation Board straight away, and next thing I knew they were here measuring the bathroom. Apparently it has to be some number of cubic feet or other before students can use it; but anyway, it is, and they told me what I should charge her, and I am. And she's paying it,' Imogen finished, as if this were some kind of a trump-card.

'*Paying* it? Then you'll *never* get rid of her. Ever!' cried Cynthia, in altruistic horror: and once again Imogen felt like saying, Look who's talking.

*

It was true, though. Piggy was a tenant now, and virtually immovable. So, for all practical purposes, was Cynthia. Imogen looked thoughtfully at the trap which had so quietly closed over her, and wondered, as many another landlady has done, how exactly she got into it.

A landlady. On top of being a widow, a stepmother, and a mother-in-law—a *landlady*. The lot.

That afternoon, she decided to take Vernon and Timmie for a walk, along the river, right away from the town to the meadows where, in May, the cowslips would be growing. Of late, she had found in herself a craving to go outside the house, to make acquaintance again with the outdoors as if it was a long neglected friend; to feel the cold air against her skin, to raise her face to the weak winter sun.

It was as if she was owed some sun; repayment for those golden autumn days after Ivor's death which she had spent indoors, hiding away from the light, while beyond the windows the loveliest October in living memory blazed and waned.

Lost sunshine. Wasted glory. The arrears can never really be made up. Even at the time, when she could not bear even to look out through a sunlit window, something inside her had raged against the waste and the wickedness of it, and had demanded vengeance. The sun! The sun!

That was one reason for the walk this afternoon. The other was to score off Dot. Well, not score off her exactly, but sort of get one up on her in the half-hearted battle the two of them seemed to have been waging of late. Dot had been silent and sullen at lunch, and had refused to eat any potatoes. Not (Imogen was well aware) for the sake of her figure, but for the sake of showing her stepmother that there'd been no point in cooking them in the first place. That way, the lateness of lunch would become all Imogen's fault. And serve her right. Piggy was her fault too, why couldn't she have put her foot down in the first place? There was no privacy anywhere, not even half way up the stairs.

Herbert, of course, would never be able to read all this into his wife's refusal of a helping of potatoes, but then he wasn't meant to. The message was for Imogen. It was a message that couldn't be voiced out loud just now, because Dot was supposed to be quarrelling with Herbert, and no sensible wife fights on two fronts at the same meal.

Imogen replied to the unspoken message equally deviously, by offering to take the boys out for the afternoon; thus putting Dot into the position of having either to abandon her sulks and display reasonable gratitude, or else of continuing her sulks and foregoing an afternoon without her children.

Every man has his price, and the same is true of mothers. The prospect of getting rid of their children for even an hour or two during the school holidays is like the offer of gin to an alcoholic: capitulation is certain. And so, by half past two, Dot was reclining blissfully by the fire in the sitting-room, and Imogen and the boys were off and away into the moist winter sunshine.

Already the best of the day was over, and down by the river the mist was beginning to rise. The sun shone through it like a great coppery ball, and at the river's edge the water was very black and still among the rushes. The opposite bank, with its boathouses and sloping gardens, was already almost invisible in the gathering mist.

The children for some reason were wildly excited by the outing, familiar though the route must have been to them from summer picnics and walks. They raced along the bank, yelling back and forth to each other through the mist, dabbling with sticks in the black water, and bashing at the dead, whispering winter reeds that rustled under the blows.

'Granny, can you see me?'

'Granny, was that a curlew?'

'Don't be silly, there aren't curlews in winter, are there, Granny? He's silly, isn't he, Granny?'

Eee-eeh! . . . Oooo—ooh! Bang. Thump. Squeals of embattled laughter, and Wellingtoned feet thudding away into the fog. Be careful, Imogen called out once or twice, but perfunctorily because of course they were being careful, as children usually are. And anyway, the water was only a foot or so deep here by the bank, it would be a nuisance, not a disaster. Imogen had a sudden, invigorating sense of knowing which was which as she'd never known it before. It was like discovering in oneself a new and unsuspected talent.

*

Naturally, she'd realised that the cowslips wouldn't be out in January, but it was a strange feeling, all the same. While the boys raced flailing into the thickening whiteness, their Wellingtons crackling on the rough, tussocky grass already stiffening with frost, Imogen stood quite still at the edge of the meadow, remembering.

*

A summer afternoon—lots and lots of summer afternoons, actually, but by now all rolled into one and indistinguishable; and evenings, too—the long, lingering June evenings—and Ivor's voice urging them—herself, that is, and whatever distinguished visitor was with them—to shush! Listen!

A cuckoo, was it? A nightingale? Some such nostalgic bird, anyway, rarely heard in these technological days; and Ivor priding himself on its existence as if he had preserved it with his own hands—created it, indeed, all by himself, in the morning of the world. You should come here at midnight, he'd say . . . at dawn . . . at mid-summer . . . and you'd hear this and this, I'd show you that and that. Nowhere else in England . . . only in the last week of June . . . . It was like God showing you round the Garden of Eden.

And the cowslips. The visitors—especially the American visitors—would be told of the custom which still flourished in Ivor's student days—thirty—forty years ago. How they would come down here in punts, on Mayday, at sunrise, and the girls would pick cowslips and make them into cowslip balls. Cowslip balls; and punting slowly back along the river in the growing light, the ripples around the pole first black and silver, and then reddening with the coming of the morning.

Typical of Ivor to have been young at such a time, and to have escaped into adulthood in the nick of time, just when it all ended, never to return.

Cowslips. Cuckoos. Summer noonday. Imogen could believe in none of it. She shivered, and glancing up from the dry, feathery winter grass, she became aware, with quite a little shock, that the mist was thickening, the pale disc of the sun was quite gone. Evening was upon them.

'Vernon! Timmie!' she called; and her voice sounded muffled and strange, bleating weakly into the fog.

They heard it, though, and came ambling into her field of vision, slower now, and growing quarrelsome, their whiny voices like seagulls. They were tired, she'd kept them out too long. She should have set off for home with them long ago.

'I'm cold, Granny, my hands are cold,' complained Vernon, dangling a pair of sodden gloves for her inspection:

'I told you so—messing about in the water all the way here,' Imogen snapped back—quite unjustly, for she hadn't told them any such thing; playing with the water had looked like a nice, thoroughly enjoyable game while the sun was still shining and no one was tired.

Altogether, it was a dispirited little party that began to straggle back along the river path by which they had set out so cheerily a couple of hours ago.

'Come *on*, both of you. It's getting dark.'

'Granny, my foot hurts . . . .'

'Granny, *wait* for me . . . .'

The children whined, Imogen nagged, and the white mist gathered thicker and damper all about them: and presently, through the dull squelch of Wellingtons and the weak twitter of childish bickering, Imogen became aware of another sound: footsteps following behind them on the river path. The owner of the footsteps was still invisible through the fog, but he (or possibly she) was gaining on them.

Imogen's first feeling was one of relief. A stranger, a small happening, has a magical effect on squabbling children—not to mention irritable adults. 'Nasty evening,' the newcomer would say as he drew level: or, 'Fog's coming down, isn't it?' and, 'Yes, isn't it?' she'd answer, in a friendly, pleasant voice. By the time the stranger had overtaken them and disappeared into the mist ahead, everyone would be feeling better. 'Who was that?' the boys would say, having to stop quarrelling to say it: and 'Why?' one of them would doubtless add as soon as she had given her necessarily vague answer.

She slowed her steps a little, the sooner to bring the therapeutic little encounter into being.

The voice, when it came, was, as she had expected, a masculine one; the first words, though, took her completely by surprise.

'Good afternoon, Mrs Barnicott,' it said, and a slight, ill-kempt figure loomed out of the mist and drew level. 'You remember me, I expect . . . I'm sure you do. I'm Teri . . . .'

He was, too. Hair a little flatter, face pale and unhealthy-looking in the drained light. Myrtle's pinky-orangey lighting had been kinder. The voice was recognisable, too, but only just, for all the shyness and diffidence had gone out of it. It was a harshly confident voice now, laced with contempt, and with a sort of secret triumph. Imogen felt Vernon's hand stealing into hers.

'Oh, hullo, Terr—Teri,' she replied, trying to put the spelling of the tiresome word into her voice, as he himself so wearyingly did. 'And what brings *you* here?' she added, trying to sound light and casual still in spite of the uneasiness growing inside her. Something in his voice, his sly cockiness, constituted a threat of some kind.

By now, the whole party had come to a standstill. With her free hand, she reached out for Timmie. Hand in hand, the little threesome faced the stranger, already in battle order though as yet no battle had been declared.

For several seconds Teri did not answer, but it was plain that the delay betokened no uncertainty or hesitation on his part. Rather he seemed to be savouring his hidden triumph, seeking to enjoy to the full these moments of secret anticipation.

'I've been following you,' he said at last, with a sort of smug superiority. 'All the way along by the river. I saw you start out. You didn't know, did you?'

Yes I did, Imogen longed to say, just to deprive him of at least this nugget of self-congratulation: but it would be foolish to provoke the man before knowing what weapons he had hidden there behind his flat, wary eyes, or beneath his dirty sweater. Especially must she go carefully with the little boys here, clinging to her in utter confidence. They knew that something was wrong—she could feel it in the clutch of their hands and by the way they weren't fidgeting—but they knew too—being only seven and eight—that Granny was all-powerful, and that it would all end in getting home comfortably for tea by the fire. With crumpets, perhaps, and chocolate biscuits. They waited: and Imogen waited: and for long seconds Teri waited. You could see that he was making the most of a moment for which he had waited for a long, long time, perhaps all his life: the moment of power.

'I've got proof, Mrs Barnicott,' he said at last, and almost reluctantly—unwilling, perhaps, to lose for ever these anticipatory moments, to exchange them for the mere fulfilment of his dream. 'I have actual proof now, you know, I hadn't when I telephoned you, though I knew I'd get it in the end. And now I have. From the hotel, Mrs Barnicott. The Hotel Magnifique. Does that ring any bells? Does it, Mrs Barnicott?'

*

The Hotel Magnifique. The hotel where Ivor would have been staying that night if he hadn't gone off and died instead, without even cancelling his booking. Gone off in his car, in the middle of the night, without a word to anybody. Intending, presumably, to drive home through the night. It was in a homeward direction, more or less, that the car had hurtled slantwise off the motorway, across the grass verge, and smashed into an ancient oak. The Talking Oak, the Sacred Oak of Dodona, whose leaves were said to be softly talking all summer long for those that had ears to hear. Had Ivor heard them, in those last seconds of his life?

He'd have liked that.

'I *heard* them—the first man to hear them in more than two thousand years!'—already the flamboyant, after-dinner anecdote would have been taking shape in his brain just as darkness smashed into it for ever.

'It's no good acting dumb, Mrs B.,' Teri upbraided her—and Imogen realised that she must have been staring vacantly, not answering his question, for several seconds—'It's no good playing silly-fools with me. You know the Hotel Magnifique all right, oh yes you do. Should do, shouldn't you, seeing you were there the night your husband died? They *saw* you. The reception clerk saw you, and so did one of the waiters. You were at the reception desk just before midnight, phoning up to the Prof.'s room. It's no good denying it, because they saw you. I've talked to both of them, I have proof . . . .'

Such a farrago of untruth restored Imogen's power of speech. Lies so blatantly unfounded, so easily refuted, were surely no threat to anybody?

'Don't be silly,' she said, 'How could they have seen me? I wasn't there. Everyone knows I wasn't. I was at home, two hundred miles away. I told you—'

'Sure you did! Like you told everybody. Well, you would, wouldn't you? And don't think I don't sympathise with you, Mrs B., I'd have done the same myself in your position. Like, I mean, no one wants to be run-in for murder, do they? And don't worry, Mrs B., no one will be—not if you act like a sensible woman and listen to me. I haven't told the police yet, what I know, and I won't do, if you'll just do a couple of small things for me. One's to do with money, I'm afraid—' he pronounced the word 'money' with a certain distaste, as one who has been brought up in such aristocratic circles that money is just not mentioned: 'Not an *awful* lot of money, Mrs B., and anyway, you're a rich woman now, aren't you, widow of the famous Prof. and all that bit. Rich enough, anyway . . . .'

'You're crazy!' Imogen interrupted. She was almost laughing at the absurdity of it all. 'Why *on earth* should I give you money when there's not the slightest shadow of truth in any of it? I mean *really* . . . '. She gave a little laugh.

Teri scowled.

'So it's funny, is it? Funny ha-ha? O.K., so it's funny. But I don't think, Mrs B., that you've quite got the hang of where we're at: what my idea is, kind of thing. This idea of mine, I've had it for a long time, actually; how maybe a person could lay hands on quite a bit of money simply by finding out about some crime the police don't know about, and then making a bargain with the criminal not to give him away if he'll . . .'

'Blackmail, you mean?' interrupted Imogen, with a little lift of the eyebrows. Did this youth really not know the word? 'On the Science side, isn't he?' Robin had said witheringly. She laughed again.

'O.K., so it's funny. It'll be funnier still, won't it, when I get to the police station. I'll have them in fits, won't I, when I tell them how Mrs-Respectable-Bloody-Barnicott did her husband in. The poor broken-hearted widow of the poor old bloody Prof., and she did him in herself. It'll have them rolling in the aisles, don't you think . . . ?'

'Tell him to go away, Granny!' suddenly pleaded Vernon—and she could feel that the cold hands of which he had so recently been complaining were now hot and sweaty—'Tell him to go away! Go away!—' with sudden, tremulous defiance he turned upon the intruder and raised his slightly quavering voice. 'Go away, please! Go away and stop bothering our grandmother!'

'Yes, she's our grandmother,' confirmed Timmie, as if this was indeed the clinching argument in the dispute. 'Come on, Granny, let's go home . . . .'

'Yes, Granny, let's go . . . .'

Both of them were tugging at her now, and, touched almost

to tears by their valiant attempt to protect her against whatever it was that was so mysteriously attacking, she gave in willingly. Hand in hand, walking briskly (no, darlings, don't run, we mustn't run) the three marched off into the fog with a fine display of dignity. For a little way, Teri padded along behind them, throwing out threats and comments almost at random.

'You'll see!' he called darkly: and, 'You think I haven't got proof but I have!' 'You'll be sorry, just see if you're not!' 'Just you wait!'

'Don't answer,' Imogen murmured to her charges. She feared that the kindergarten style of the challenge might inspire retaliation in kind, and thus lead to a resumption of dialogue.

'Don't answer—just keep walking,' she urged them. 'If he sees we're taking no notice, he'll soon get tired of it . . . .'

Surprisingly, this was just what happened. After another couple of minutes, the footsteps behind them flagged, then fell silent as their owner swerved suddenly off the path and on to the grass alongside the sports ground, which offered a shortcut into the town.

'There was someone else saw you, too,' was his parting shot as the white fog closed over him. 'Someone you know very, very well.'

'Shush!' whispered Imogen to her companions, trying to nip in the bud any item of appropriate repartee that might be occurring to them. 'Don't say anything—pretend you haven't heard.'

And only now, safely out of range of their tormentor, did the three venture to break into a run.

There *were* crumpets for tea. The children had been quite right. Everyone was back safely, and the dining-room fire was blazing, just as they had known it would be. Routine had emerged triumphant, as it usually does, in the face of almost anything. It takes more than a Teri to make people miss their tea.

He had achieved something, though—something which would no doubt have pleased him, could he have known about it. Before the second lot of crumpets were out of the toaster, he had grown nearly seven feet tall, his voice was like that of Marty the Monster in Timmie's favourite comic, and his eyes were as big as saucers.

'All evil they was, and his glance was like forked lightning,' Timmie elaborated fluently, 'and he glared at us like . . . like . . .'—here either Timmie's memory or his library of clichés faltered, for 'Like anything' he finished, a little lamely. Then, as if to make up for the momentary lapse, he resumed yet more shrilly:

'Ever so big he was, almost a giant. And when he came at us . . . Oooh!'

It was at this point that Uncle Robin left the table with a groan of boredom, carrying his teacup with him; but the response of the rest of the company was splendid. Cynthia, her blue eyes very wide, was giving excited little squeals in all the right places, while Dot, looking both anxious and smug, was nodding her head sagely at every other sentence, as if cheeking-off Timmie's complexes against some ideal list lodged in the back of her mind. Even Piggy, who had condescended this afternoon to drink a cup of ordinary, non-herbal tea with the rest of the household, was looking vaguely interested for once. The only member of the party to be wholly unimpressed by the recital was Vernon.

'No, he didn't,' 'No, it wasn't,' 'No, it was *me* who said that,' he kept interposing, but of course no one listened. He hadn't really expected them to, for it was always like this. He, Vernon, always remembered much more accurately than Timmie did what had actually happened on any occasion, and could have explained it all properly, in precise and consecutive detail, but unfortunately not so that anyone would actually ever listen. If *he'd* been relating this afternoon's adventure, he'd have got it all absolutely right, and they'd *all* have been bored, not just Uncle Robin. His father would have carried on with his crossword puzzle without even looking up; his mother would have said Was it, dear? Well I never, and gone on with her argument about tea-bags being cheaper in the long run; and 'Auntie' Cynthia (whose puff-ball blondeness and tinkling jewellery Vernon greatly and secretly admired) would have sighed, and looked at her watch, and asked Dot if it wasn't the children's bedtime?

It wasn't, of course. It hardly ever was when Cynthia asked the question, but she remained hopeful. It wasn't that she disliked children particularly—in fact, if challenged, she would probably have claimed to be a child-lover. It was just their company that she couldn't stand. And most of all she couldn't stand it when their mother was around as well, nudging and grimacing, and interrupting Cynthia's best anecdotes with mouthings and whisperings about them being 'unsuitable'.

Well, of course they were. How boring can you get? Conversation fit for an eight-year-old isn't fit to listen to, that was Cynthia's credo, and she found it frustrating in the extreme to have her narrative style thus cramped by Dot's arbitrary maternal whims. And most frustrating of all was it at this evening hour, when something like two-thirds of the household were gathered cosily round the fire in a setting absolutely perfect for tearing to shreds the characters and reputations of the other third. And those of their friends, too, and their friends-of-friends . . . . Oh, it was maddening! And all for the sake of a couple of snotty-nosed kids who didn't even need to listen if they didn't want to.

For Dot, too, the situation was fraught with problems, and she, too, suffered. For her, the problem was how to be modern and permissive as well as preventing the boys listening; and she spent many anxious hours worrying about it, and reading magazine articles on the question. The articles came up with answers, all right; confident, expert answers, based on all the latest research, but somehow with singularly little bearing on the actual problem with which Dot was currently confronted. The experts all agreed, for example, that children of Timmie's and Vernon's ages should be told frankly and truthfully about the facts of life: but did this really include telling them the details of

Cynthia's ex-boyfriend's prostate trouble? Or not? On this, as on so many similar issues, the massed company of the experts was distressingly silent; and thus Dot was left in the end to her own anxious devices, guided only by her instincts and by her passionately-held permissive principles; the most crucial one of which being that children should always be left entirely free to choose for themselves to do exactly what she, Dot, wanted them to do.

But even with an unswerving belief like this to guide her, it could still be difficult. Sex, it would appear, was liable to be just as time-consuming and unsatisfactory in Bermuda as it was in Twickenham: and Dot often found herself in a quandary about it all, not to mention increasingly resentful. Having dutifully brought up her children to believe that sex is wonderful (albeit with singularly little domestic evidence to back up the proposition), Dot was understandably reluctant to see all her painstaking work undone in a single evening by Auntie Cynthia's ill-judged anecdotes.

On this particular evening, though, things were going a bit better than usual from Dot's point of view. Timmie's burgeoning narrative, however silly, could hardly be unsuitable for his own ears; nor (she hoped) could any of the improbable recital possibly remind Cynthia of any of those event-packed days in Bermuda which always seemed to give such an unfortunate turn to any conversation. Why, they didn't even *have* fog in Bermuda, did they? Let alone fog so thick that . . . 'we couldn't see our hands in front of our faces, could we, Granny?' 'Yes we could' (this with dogged disgruntlement from Vernon), 'we could see at least four feet . . . . Actually, the visibility was . . .'

Or not. Or maybe. No one would ever know, for by now

Timmie had filled all their heads with a fog thick as cotton-wool, impervious, fact-resistant, and apparently outside time. Timmie was being Creative, Vernon recognised sourly, that's why the grownups were all sitting like paralysed guinea-pigs, no one daring to be bored first. Creativity always had this effect on people, Vernon had observed; you couldn't fight it, you just had to sit it out.

One day, he thought darkly, one of Timmie's stories will go on *for ever*; and *then* what will they do?

They'll all starve, that's what. They'll sit round and *starve*!

It didn't quite come to that.

*

'No, Cynthia dear, it's *not* their bedtime, it's barely six o'clock,' Dot was saying repressively; and 'Quarter-past, dear, actually', Cynthia was correcting her with exaggerated sweetness; while underneath, the real battle raged wordlessly between them, veering this way and that, the issue as yet undecided. Would Dot, or would she not, succeed in preventing Cynthia giving voice to the speculations already bubbling so insistently in her brain—highly 'unsuitable' ones by any standard—about Teri, and about his *real* motive for accosting two little boys in a fog . . . .

'I mean, I don't want to upset anyone—' Cynthia was gleefully beginning—and then suddenly quailed. She *did* want to upset them, of course, that was the whole point of this kind of discussion; but as a mature and sensible woman she realised that you can't always have what you want. You have to cut your coat according to your cloth. For the time being, she would have to restrict herself to the relatively innocuous aspects of the episode—murder, blackmail, and false accusation.

'You should *sue* him, Imogen,' she urged, with all the righteous fervour of the one who isn't going to have to lift a finger. 'You shouldn't let him get away with it. Get the police after him. It's libel. Or is it slander?—I'm not sure, but I do know you get much more money for one than the other, I forget which. I once knew a woman in Hamilton who got 18,000 dollars just for someone saying her hair was dyed. And it was, too . . . .'

*

Her voice jerked into silence. The dining-room door slammed open, crashing against the rim of the antique sideboard in a way that would have appalled Ivor if he hadn't been dead, and would have set him re-telling all through dinner the story of how he'd picked up that sideboard in Penzance, buying it for a song from a chap who thought he was Napoleon and wanted to make amends for all the evil he'd done in the world. How Ivor's acquiring of an eighteenth-century oak sideboard for a tenth of its market price could be said to have compensated the world in any degree for the depredations of the Napoleonic wars, was never made clear; but then it didn't need to be. Because, of course, the story wasn't about Napoleon at all, nor about the poor madman, nor even about the sideboard itself. It was about Ivor, and how he attracted to himself bizarre and exciting adventures wherever he went. That was the point of the story; it didn't need a moral as well.

The dully painful crack of wood on antique wood died away, and there stood Robin, in the doorway. Smiling, as he always smiled when something was going badly wrong. Was Imogen the only member of the little party who recognised the signs? She sat very still, clutching the edge of her chair.

Yes, here it came: the witty, off-hand, joking remark. Robin deadly serious at last: Robin angry as he had only been once or twice before in his life.

'Piggy, darling,' he said lightly, 'Shall I tell you what's new? Somebody wants you. Wants *you*! Only on the telephone, as it happens, but we all have to start somewhere.'

And as Piggy, mouth open, reacting at last to her environment (as flatworms, protozoa and sea-snails have always been accustomed to do), got noisily to her feet, Robin stood quietly watching her.

'Boyfriend trouble, from the sound of it, darling,' he observed silkily, holding the door open for her with exaggerated courtesy, 'Congratulations'—and turning on his heel he followed her swiftly out of the room, closing the door behind him.

Funny, thought Imogen. I didn't hear the telephone ring. Were we all talking too loud—too preoccupied to notice it? Out of curiosity, and a mounting sense of unease, she made an excuse to go out to the kitchen . . . more hot water . . . fresh tea . . . . Teapot in hand, she slipped out of the room and made her way, as slowly as she dared, across the hall.

'No,' she heard Piggy saying in a low voice on the telephone. 'No, well, I haven't had a chance, have I?' And then—in a little spurt of indignation: 'Oh, for Heaven's sake, *you're* the one who . . . No. No, of course I didn't, how could I? I keep telling you . . . Oh, don't be so *stupid*! It's all very well for *you*, you don't know what it's *like* here . . . .'

The response at the other end of the line sounded like a terrier yapping, frustrated and frantic at the mouth of a rabbit-hole. Imogen could not in decency loiter any longer, so she passed on into the kitchen, boiled up the kettle, re-filled the teapot; and by the time she came to make her return journey, the telephoning was all over. It was only much later in the evening that Piggy was found to be crying, bitterly and uncontrollably.

On the stairs, of course, so that no one could go up to bed without being either heartlessly indifferent or tactlessly interfering.

'No, I'm all right,' 'No, thank you, it's nothing,' were the sort of replies received by would-be comforters, and by midnight even Cynthia had given up. In general, Cynthia rather fancied herself in the rôle of confidante to those in trouble—and indeed, in a way she was rather well-qualified for it. For one thing, she really enjoyed trouble, provided it was only somebody else's; and for another, her range of experience was, in its way, formidable. You name it, somebody she knew had had it. In matters of masculine villainy she was by way of being a world expert, and could hold her own, Rat for Rat, in discourse with any woman in the land.

But on this occasion, the result of all her efforts was rather disappointing. Either she was applying the wrong methods, or else Piggy didn't have the right troubles.

'Leave me alone!' the girl kept saying; and then, in a sudden spurt of anger: 'Oh, for God's sake, can't you all stop spying on me? Creeping about the house on tiptoe . . . peeping in at me through windows . . . . I'm sick and tired of it! What the hell do you think you're going to discover, anyway . . . ?'

Afterwards, calming down a little, she conceded, grudgingly, that she hadn't meant Cynthia herself. 'It's certain *other* people in this house,' she explained darkly, and had refused to be further drawn.

'Oh, *please* go away,' she'd repeated: and at last, with some chagrin, and an aching back from squatting matily on the third step of the stairs for so long, Cynthia had done so, going off to impart her meagre findings to whoever might still be up. Dot and Imogen, as it happened, were the only two available, Herbert having slunk guiltily off to bed before anything could become his fault, and Robin having locked himself in his room with a KEEP OUT notice on the door and his record-player blaring away inside.

And so it happened that Dot and Imogen were the only two to hear of the encounter, and even they didn't hear very much. Being low on facts, as well as weary, Cynthia made it short. That Piggy's boyfriend had found another girl, gone to prison, become impotent, forgotten Piggy's birthday, expected her to pay for her own dinner, was Cynthia's theory: and with the whole mystery thus satisfactorily solved, everyone could at last relax and go to bed.

Or almost. There was still one small obstacle to be surmounted.

'I'll never be able to get Herbert up by seven,' complained Dot, yawning hugely, and pausing on the bend of the stairs to hear the murmur of sympathy that should, by rights, come her way.

It didn't. Not because either Cynthia or Imogen were being wilfully unsympathetic; it was just that it was all so complicated. Dot and Herbert's morning routine (so far as Imogen could make it out) seemed to go something like this: the alarm went at six-forty-five, and thereupon Dot proceeded to wake Herbert in time for him to wake her in time for her to nag him into bringing the cup of tea which was essential for enabling her to wake up sufficiently to wake him in time to eat his breakfast and catch his train.

It was all too much, especially at this time of night; and so 'good night' was all that any of them said, and Dot plodded off to bed with a familiar sense of being vaguely disappointed, vaguely let-down. The sense of grievance was so vague, and so familiar, that she scarcely noticed it. Almost, it gave her a sense of security, like an old and well-worn dressing-gown wrapped about her.

12

It must have been between two and three in the morning when Imogen was suddenly awakened, and she knew at once that what had woken her was something out of the past. Something familiar.

A voice? A touch? Too sleepy to be frightened, she lay quietly, waiting for it to happen again.

'Mummy! Mummy!'

The voice rang up through the floor of her attic room and jolted her wide awake, her mind a-whirl with the old familiar conflict: to interfere, or not to interfere? 'Mummy', the child had called, not 'Daddy', or 'Granny'; and this put everyone in a spot. For it so happened that Mummy combined an acute sense of the sanctity of motherhood with a remarkable capacity for sleeping like the dead through absolutely anything. Both interference and non-interference got you into almost exactly equal degrees of trouble.

'Mummy!'

Imogen sat up, and listened intently, hoping any moment to hear the irritable flip-flop of Dot's slippers along the corridor below. Mummy, I've been sick. Mummy, my eiderdown's disappeared. Mummy, he says I'm a . . . . No I didn't, yes he did . . .

But it wasn't happening. No peevish sing-song of grievance and reproof floated up through the wooden floor. There was one moment when, in the waiting silence, she thought she had caught the sound of Dot's footsteps; but she couldn't have, for almost at once the darkness rocked with an absolute crescendo of screaming.

'Mummy! Daddy! Granny!'

Such an unselective volley of desperation could be ignored no longer. In a matter of seconds, Imogen was out of bed, down the twisting attic stairs, and racing along the corridor below, thickly carpeted and almost silent beneath her bare, running feet.

'Timmie? Vernon?'

She stepped softly into the room, fell over the electric train set, recovered herself, and peered anxiously towards the shadowy scaffolding of bunks at the far end of the room. She didn't turn the light on, not wishing to rouse whichever one it was that wasn't crying; not that the precaution was really necessary: like most children, Timmie and Vernon tended to sleep peacefully through one another's shrieks and screams.

'What is it?' she whispered, beginning to pick her way cautiously across the littered, glimmering floor. 'What's the matter?'

No answer. The room was bright with moonlight through the uncurtained windows, and she could see clearly the humps of the small bodies under the blankets—both, at the moment quite motionless. No telling which was which, either, as they were in the habit of taking 'turns' with the top bunk each night—usually with much shrieking and squabbling. Vernon, in his systematic way, would make lists, for days ahead, of which bunk would be whose each night: but it never worked. 'Sunday doesn't count, because I was feeling sick,' Timmie would resourcefully argue: or, 'You swopped your Wednesday turn for my two-colour biro, don't you remember?'—and battle would be joined; Vernon, list in hand, shrieking out the claims of justice, reason, and the written contract, while Timmie, bland and giggling, would clamber on to the coveted bunk and prepare for the assault.

And so when the dark shape in the bottom bunk lurched suddenly into a sitting position and began to sob, Imogen still couldn't tell with any certainty which of them it was.

Except that of course it was Vernon. This sort of thing always was. Even when they were toddlers, it had always been he, not Timmie, who had had the nightmares, and the stomach-aches, and had heard the wolves howling in the wind. But it hadn't happened for some time now—not for a couple of years at least—and everyone had assumed he had grown out of it.

*

A face. Not a wolf at all. He had dreamed of a face leaning over him and staring down at him as he slept. As is the way of nightmares, nothing much had actually happened: the face had not even scowled, or uttered threatening words: but the aura of terror accompanying the apparition was something which Vernon could find no vocabulary to describe.

'So awful Granny . . . so awful!' he kept repeating. He babbled of lips shining wet in the moonlight: of a wet, shining chin, bristly; and wild hair dangling. The face had come nearer as he lay in the paralysis of nightmare; he had smelt its breath as it tried to speak. It was saying something, telling him something, but the syllables were nonsense syllables, and he could not understand. He could feel the spit, though, sputtering from the consonants: he could feel it still, he could, he could! Desperately, he scrubbed at his cheeks with his fists, with his blankets . . . .

'Feel it, Granny, *feel* it!' he sobbed. 'Feel my face, it's all wet! *Is* it, Granny? Is it all wet?'

Gently, reassuring, she stroked the flushed cheeks. They were wet, all right, but that was with crying, and with the sweat of fear.

'It's all right, darling, it was only a dream. It's all right . . . Granny's here . . . .'

He was a baby again, clinging to her with the despairing, infantile strength of any baby primate, dragging her down, pinioning her against the pillow.

'. . . Only a dream, Granny? It *was* only a dream, wasn't it?' he pleaded, his body shuddering beneath the blankets; and 'Of course it was!' she kept answering him, over and over again.

*

Only a dream. Only a dream. At last she felt his trembling subside; the arms around her neck released their grip, and he was a baby no longer, but eight years old, and drawing politely away from her.

'Yes, of course, Granny. Yes, I know,' he agreed, his brow puckered with concentration in the moonlight. 'It must have been a dream, mustn't it, because a person's face couldn't really be like that, could it? All staring, and not talking properly, and with eyes as big as saucers . . . .'

*

So that was it. Damn Timmie and his eternal melodramas, giving his brother nightmares like this. As if the encounter on the river bank hadn't been quite upsetting enough in the first place—the more so, of course, since no sensible adult explanation of it all had subsequently been forthcoming. Imogen blamed herself for not having given the children some simple, reassuring answer—but how could she when there wasn't one? Adult omniscience had cracked, and this is a state of affairs more frightening to children than any amount of danger.

Still the crisis seemed to be over now.

'I was silly, wasn't I, Granny?' said Vernon smugly, pulling the covers up to his chin; and when she offered to stay with him till he fell asleep, he shook his head.

'No, thank you, Granny. I'm O.K. now.' He looked small and vulnerable on his moon-drenched pillow, and she hesitated.

'I'm O.K.,' he repeated. 'It was only a dream, wasn't it? A silly dream.'

Good night, then, darling.

Good night. Granny.

Sleep well.

Good night. Good night.

*

And then—less than a minute later, and before Imogen had even reached the head of the stairs—scream after scream, such as she had never heard or imagined:

'Granny! *Granny*! GRANNY!'

13

This time, the whole house was awakened. Along they came flocking, pale and ramshackle in the moonlight, clutching their pyjama-cords and their half-donned dressing gowns, and gathered in the doorway of the boys' room.

What is it? What's happened? Why? How do you mean?—while Vernon, half-hysterical with fear, lay face downward on his pillow, choking and sobbing.

'No . . . . No . . . !' he gasped once, when Dot, leaning solicitously over the bed, asked him where it hurt? Enthusiastic though Dot was about psychological explanations in general, at night-time she preferred something that could be silenced with an aspirin. Herbert, tweaking futilely at her sleeve and murmuring, 'Let *me* . . .' got the full brunt of her bewilderment.

Peppermints! That bag of peppermint bullseyes Herbert had passed round yesterday evening—*that* was the cause of it all! Peppermints on an empty stomach—well, all right, a *full* one, then, don't quibble—peppermints were well known to cause . . .

Well, to cause . . .

To cause whatever it was that Vernon had got, for Heaven's sake. That's what peppermints were well known to cause: and if only Herbert had had the faintest understanding of his own child . . . .

Meanwhile Cynthia, a fluttering vision of whitely moonlit hair and floating negligée, had undertaken to ring the doctor; in less than a minute she was back again to ask what his telephone number was, she couldn't find it in the local directory; and did he spell his name Grieves or Greives?

He'll never turn out at this hour of the night, predicted Herbert: and drugs, drugs, drugs, I don't believe in drugs countered Dot, as if contradicting him. By this time, Piggy too was in the doorway, blinking and censorious, and wanting to know if something had happened? On being told that it had, she shrugged contemptuously and departed, apparently satisfied.

By now, Dot and Herbert, united by anxiety for their eldest child, were locked in deadly, *sotto voce* combat about who it was who hadn't bought any aspirins last Saturday; while Cynthia, ping-pinging away on the telephone downstairs really seemed settled for the night. 'It couldn't be GREAVES, could it?' she shouted up the stairs once; and on receiving no clear answer went back, apparently happily, to her dialling. '*Who?*' she would squeal occasionally, on a startled yelp; or 'But I thought . . . Oh, I'm *so* sorry . . .', and then, nothing daunted, would try again. Of all the neighbourhood, Imogen reflected, only the doctor could be sleeping peacefully that night. Robin, of course, had been no trouble at all right from the start. He'd just looked in once and remarked 'Oh, Christ!' and gone away again.

And in the midst of all this turmoil the prime mover of it all crouched, white-faced and almost unnoticed on his bunk, waiting for someone to make it not have happened.

They got the story out of him at last—Dot, Herbert, and Imogen between them—and it was no wonder he had been so scared. It is no joke to have the same nightmare twice in the space of a few minutes, falling back into it the moment you close your eyes, for all the world as if it had been there all the time, quietly waiting.

'And I didn't even know I was asleep,' Vernon sobbed. 'I thought you'd only just gone out of the room, Granny . . . I just shut my eyes, and opened them again, and it was *there*. Just like before . . . sort of looking down at me . . . and sort of talking . . . and oh, Granny, Mummy, this time it had *teeth* . . . .'

It must have had them in the previous dream, of course, or Vernon would have remarked on it being toothless. But Imogen could guess what it was he was trying to describe. It was what teeth look like when the lips are drawn back from them in laughter, or in horror. Yellow teeth in the moonlight, long and sharp they must have seemed to Vernon, for here he was describing them as 'fangs', and from the wet, loose lips the slobber had hung in strings, swinging, as the face came nearer. He had tried to scream . . . to hit out . . . and then, suddenly, he *was* screaming, *was* hitting out . . . and the terrible face was gone.

*

Two aspirins, Dot decided, and a cup of hot milk. While she went in quest of these remedies, driving Herbert before her like a delinquent hen, Imogen stayed sitting on Vernon's bunk and assuring him all over again that yes, of course it was only a dream, and that no, of course he wouldn't dream it again, nobody ever dreams the same dream more than twice.

'Don't they really, Granny? Not ever?'

Vernon's interest seemed to have been caught by this tendentious piece of arithmetic, and Imogen found herself having to assemble impromptu bits of supporting evidence from far and wide, starting with the Bible. Soon, to make him smile, she was telling him of various silly dreams *she* had had in the course of her life—carefully-selected dreams, of course, about kittens, and the seaside, and headmistresses bicycling up lamp-posts.

Vernon listened gratefully, smiling sometimes, seeing through his step-grandmother's rather transparent intentions, but nevertheless trying to go along with it all. Trying to be bamboozled, to be manœuvred out of the darkness and the terror, and to be palmed off with the light of common day.

Only a dream. Only a dream. By the time Dot came back with the hot milk and the aspirin, Vernon seemed to be quite tranquil again, though inclined to be argumentative about the milk.

'No, that's not skin, it's cream, it'll do you good,' Dot admonished him; and then, to Imogen: 'Why don't you go off to bed, Imogen, and get some sleep? There's nothing more you can do, he'll be fine now, he'll have forgotten all about it by the morning. Now, come on, dear, drink it up . . . .'

Milk. The Milk of Forgetfulness. Dot was pouring it into him like petrol into a car, confident of getting results.

Would he forget, though? From the bottom of her heart, Imogen willed that it should be so. Willed him to forget the nightmare; to forget all the fuss and commotion it had caused. And, above all, to forget that moment when his eyes had met hers, and she had known, and he knew that she had known, that it hadn't been a dream at all. It had happened.

14

R eal? With things that have happened during the night,
it is sometimes hard to tell. The coming of the morning
does something to them, like light getting into a camera. Imogen lay staring at the square of yellow dawn across from her
bed, and was amazed at how little perturbed she now felt. She
had gone back to bed after all the excitement not expecting
to sleep at all—not, indeed, intending to, so puzzled was she,
and so fearful of what might happen next. Strange, terrifying
possibilities had swirled together in her mind, foregathering
noisily, like a football crowd in an ugly mood: and next thing
she knew, it was morning, and the whole thing just looked silly.

*

A cruel trick of some kind? Masks? Dressing-up? These were
the lines on which her last conscious thoughts had been moving; but now, by the light of day, it all seemed preposterous.
Who would be capable of such senseless cruelty towards a small
boy, and what for?

Robin? He, of course (so he often boasted), was capable of
anything; but only if it was convenient. 'Unselfish cruelty isn't

my thing,' he'd have pointed out, explaining to her that wickedness, like anything else, has to be made to pay.

Piggy, then? *Her* qualifications for the deed were simply that no one knew anything about her at all. This by itself would surely never have got her a job as, say, a computer-programmer, and so why should it be held to qualify her for so complex and specialised an act of villainy as had been perpetrated last night?

The rest of the household would seem to be out of the question. Unless, perhaps, Timmie . . . ? A piece of childish, melodramatic idiocy? Imogen cast her mind back. Apart from a brief feeling of thankfulness that his brother's yells didn't seem to be waking him, Imogen hadn't thought about Timmie at all last night, or even looked in the top bunk to make sure he was there. He *could* . . . Yes, he just could, as some kind of silly joke . . . but surely not without a lot of subsequent giggling and horseplay and general showing off? He would never have slipped unobtrusively out of sight, claiming no credit for all the drama and uproar. Not *Timmie* . . . .

The square of light brightened under the impact of the morning, and Imogen felt the whole problem slipping from her grasp, like something you are trying to fish out of a drain, scooping and prodding feebly with bent sticks against the slithery sides. And now, reassuring as bird-calls, she began to hear the sound of quarrelling in the room below:

'No, it's *my* go, you've had your go!'

'It isn't, shut up, it's not fair! *I* found it . . . .'

Eeeeee! Ooooooo! Thump. Thud. Brrumph.

So all was well. Imogen sighed with relief. Whatever it was

that had upset Vernon during the night, it was plain that by this morning he had quite recovered.

Not so Herbert's umbrella. After serving as a parachute in commando raids off the top bunk for nearly an hour before breakfast, it just wasn't quite the umbrella it had been; and poor Herbert, after a brief and fruitless struggle with its mysterious disorder of the spokes, went dismally off to catch his train without it, protecting himself as best he could from the wintry downpour by clutching over his head an un-read copy of *The Times*. The thought of the sodden crossword puzzle, untouched, and growing more and more illegible, saddened him, but he hadn't dared scold the boys as another father might because Dot was still going on about the peppermints; and you never knew. After all, little research has actually been done on the effect of peppermints on umbrella spokes, and Herbert liked to be on the safe side.

*

Herbert off to work, with all the other commuting husbands: Dot on the phone about the re-covering of an eiderdown: the boys squabbling idly about the dinosaur on the cornflake packet. As normal a slice of family life as you could hope to witness, Imogen thought warily, scenting problems as a deer scents danger.

All this normality was getting a bit much. It was beginning to seem altogether too settled, too permanent. How long *were* they planning to stay? They'd come for Christmas, and now here they were on—what was it?—January 11th, and still not a word about leaving. Admittedly, the visit had purported to be for Imogen's sake, a deed of mercy, undertaken out of the goodness of Dot's heart—at the thought that goodness and mercy *might* follow her all the days of her life—and certainly would if Edith and Dot had their way—Imogen gave a little, involuntary shudder. She decided to speak to Dot this very morning, and pin her down to a definite date of departure.

Dot was not an easy person to pin down. It wasn't so much that she evaded one's questions as that she answered them so precisely that in the end one rather lost the gist of the thing.

No, there was no great hurry about getting back to Twickenham, not actually. Everything was under control, and no, she and Herbert weren't missing any New Year parties or anything, Twickenham wasn't like that. No, Herbert wasn't finding the travelling too much of a strain, not really. Sixty-five minutes on the mainline train wasn't really any more strain than crossing London by Tube in the rush-hour; less, if anything, thank you very much for thinking of it all the same.

The children's school? Well, term hadn't started yet, had it? And anyway, missing a bit of school doesn't do a child any harm, not at this age. Besides, that Fawley Road school wasn't the only school in the world, was it? In fact, if Imogen wanted her to be quite, quite frank, Dot had never really thought much of that school in the first place: all that Baby Jesus stuff, and plimsolls kept in the desks—unhygienic, in Dot's opinion. Not enough emphasis on art, either, you'd think they would at least have clay modelling . . . .

Imogen found herself agreeing with everything, and no further on at all. That was the trouble about discussing anything with Dot: with every exchange of question and answer, the next move became increasingly unclear. The only thing less productive than a discussion with Dot was a discussion with Herbert, which was like cornering a rabbit, and made you feel both heartless and ineffectual.

And in any case, it wasn't precisely that Imogen didn't *want* Dot and her family staying here. In some ways it was rather nice, and provided a sort of impromptu barricade against the Future, that arch-enemy of all new widows. Suddenly, she realised that this, actually, was what the whole random, untidy set-up of her present household was all about. All these temporary, ill-assorted people—Cynthia, Piggy and the rest—had arrived as reinforcements in a life-and-death battle that she had not realised she was waging. They had formed around her a tight little makeshift garrison protecting her against ever having to decide anything at all about anything.

If only they could be temporary permanently. This was the paradox; difficult enough to resolve even without Dot's logic thrown in for good measure. Because the temporary carries within itself the seeds of its own destruction. If it lasts, it thereby becomes permanent, changing traitorously, under one's very eyes, into the very enemy against which it seemed to be giving protection. All those indecisions which were designed to keep the future at bay are suddenly seen to have been decisions, albeit negative ones. And—ye Gods—this is the Future. This that I've got—*now*!

Imogen began to panic a little. Dot and Herbert . . . Robin . . . Cynthia and Piggy . . . were they going to stay *for ever*? I'll have lodgers, she'd said, and there *were* lodgers. Had God, perhaps, felt like this when, not knowing His own power, He'd said 'Let there be light'?

And it wasn't just the lodgers themselves, either; for hot on the heels of lodgers come their things. Their lamp-shades and their hair-dryers and their peculiar coffee-percolators. Their tooth-brushes too, and their bottles of this and that in the bathroom . . . her home was silting up with other people's possessions; they came like sand blowing in under the door: Cynthia's sunray lamp, Herbert's galoshes, Piggy's Eat-and-Love Cook Book. And as for Dot, she'd brought just about everything: her sewing-machine, her carpet-sweeper, her special Eesi-Fold ironing board. And out there, in the hall, the alien coats were mustering, like a barbarian army at the gates. Every day there were more of them hanging on the pegs—suede coats, fur coats, battered old raincoats; coats that she'd never seen in her life before were behaving as if they *lived* here. Their owners were even becoming possessive and territorial about them. 'What's my burnous doing here, I've been looking for it for days,' Piggy had complained only yesterday, just exactly as if her wretched burnous had a *right* to be somewhere . . . . At the thought of it all, Imogen felt a sort of panic rising within her, she was actually trembling. An ailment common enough, though little recognised by orthodox psychiatry, had her in its grip: landlady-panic. The thought of all these people actually *living* here, under her roof, became terrifying. The assorted faces—anxious, kindly, self-absorbed, indifferent—began to coalesce in her mind into a single monstrous entity, an unstoppable force, nosing its way into her home, blindly and brainlessly devouring everything in its path . . . was *this* the face that Vernon had seen last night, she wildly wondered? This monstrous, collective face of take-over and destruction?

*

The Hoovering calmed her down. It is a soothing occupation, as well as noisy enough to drown one's thoughts.

Drawing-room . . . dining-room . . . Meccano-off-the-floor-please-children-yes-I-said-*now*. Hall, corridor . . . by the time she came to Ivor's study, the procedure was so automatic that she had picked up a dozen or more of the papers scattered on the carpet before she glanced at them, and realised just how strange it was that they should be there.

To start with, she had never seen them before. She had thought herself to be familiar with all of Ivor's manuscripts, past and present. Wasn't it she who had typed them, proof-read them, parcelled them up for the publisher? Who had written diplomatic letters about them, explaining why they were too long, too late, too insulting to Professor So-and-So? Even his very earliest efforts—schoolboy poems and such—had passed through her hands in one way or another; photo-copying them, pasting them into scrap-books, getting them re-printed in the Old Boys Magazine. And as for a man-uscript like this—part of a full-length book, evidently, for 'CHAPTER V' had just caught her eye at the head of one of the pages—why, she would have expected to know it almost by heart. At the very least, she'd have typed it, answered tele-phone calls about it, helped with the proof-reading.

On top of which, this wasn't a mere typed duplicate; it was

the original draft, in Ivor's looped, boldly-sloping handwriting. Ivor had always treasured his own hand-written drafts: they were part of his persona, bricks in the edifice he was building for posterity. He hated to part with them, but on the other hand there were all these American libraries always after just such scrawled originals, the messier and the more illegible the better, and there was nothing Ivor enjoyed more than playing hard-to-get across the Atlantic.

A manuscript like this would have set the bargaining going in a big way. It had taken Imogen some time to accustom herself to the idea of muddle as a marketable commodity; but having once accepted the notion, she was now quite a connoisseur, and could see at once that all these crossings-out, these looped balloons and arrows swooping incomprehensibly this way and that across the page, would have been exactly what was wanted. She *couldn't* have missed the trans-Atlantic fuss and arguing.

She *had* missed it, though. Had the whole thing been before her time, perhaps? So long before that she hadn't come in even for the revisions, and the re-printings, and the arguments about the new layout? But surely, even in that case, she would at least have *heard* of the book, seen it on the shelves? A dozen copies at least, that was Ivor's rule with his own works. What with foreign translations, paperback editions and the rest, they filled up the whole of one wall, from floor to ceiling.

Crete. Minoan Crete. That was funny, too. The Minoans weren't Ivor's subject at all, he'd never touched them. Imogen stared thoughtfully at the little clusters of strange angular-looking symbols that cropped up here and there in the text, and wondered about it more and more. Linear-B, perhaps? Ivor had never, so far as she could recall, involved himself in this controversy or in its historical repercussions; and yet here, in his own unmistakable handwriting, was a whole book—or at least a substantial section of a book—centring on this very theme. Not a textbook, either, or any kind of a hack job. This was a book written from the heart, vibrant with the sense of new discovery:

'One of the most exciting aspects of the Minos legend, and one which seems entirely to have escaped the attention of scholars to date . . .'

'To date.' Was there a clue here, perhaps? Shuffling through the untidy little bundle of pages she had by now assembled, Imogen came upon one which must have been the end-page of a chapter or section, for it was marked with the date on which it had been completed: May, 1936.

1936! Why, Ivor could have been scarcely more than an undergraduate at the time! Imogen had a sudden poignant vision of a young and as yet insignificant Ivor, his Finals already hanging over him, and yet finding the time to scribble furiously away under the summer trees, or far into the night, at his first and still-born book.

Because, of course, the book must have been a failure. How could it have been otherwise, with an author barely twenty years old pitting his wits against mature scholars all over the world? Maybe it never even found a publisher at all?

Ivor's first and only failure. No wonder he had never spoken of it. No wonder, either, if he had chucked Minoan Crete for good and all, and had embarked on the Aristophanes translations by which he had first made his name. The only wonder was that he had ever kept such a memento of failure at all.

Probably he had forgotten all about it. It must have been buried deep, under layer after layer of the accumulations of his more successful years.

Who, then, had unearthed it now, and why? It must have been among those piles of papers that had been shoved first into Dot's room and then up to the attic. If it had been here, in the study, all the time, she'd have come across it long ago.

Who, then, had brought it in here? Who could have wanted, late last night, to be messing about, all by themselves, with this ancient, yellowing, irrelevant pile of manuscript? And what, finally, could they have been doing with it that had resulted in the pages being scattered this morning all over the floor, as if a great wind had blown through the room?

15

Nobody, naturally, knew anything about it.

'Linear *what?*' said Cynthia, reaching for the salad-cream; and Dot, with her eyes fixed reproachfully on her stepmother, remarked that if only people wouldn't keep messing about with everything, then this sort of thing wouldn't happen.

'But I *wasn't.* That's the whole *point.* I'd never even *seen* the thing before,' Imogen protested; and Robin laid down his fork with a sigh and remarked that the excitement was killing him.

'*Manuscripts?* In Dad's *study?* You'll be finding soil in the garden next,' he observed: and, 'Talking of the garden,' Cynthia prattled on brightly, 'I noticed yesterday that that poor laburnum tree, which Ivor loved so much . . .'

When he wasn't threatening to chop it down, that was, for being too near the house: a sort of love, perhaps, peculiar to gardeners? But before Imogen could decide whether Cynthia's sentimental and somewhat unpredictable recollections were ever worth the contradicting, she was interrupted by Vernon, who burst suddenly and rather quietly into tears over his second helping of meat loaf.

'Minos!' he sobbed. 'Where's Minos? Why didn't we bring Minos?'

Not Minos of Crete (though no doubt the discussion about his grandfather's manuscript had reminded him of the name), but Minos of Twickenham. Minos the ginger Tom, who had been part of the Twickenham household since before Vernon was born—had, indeed, been taken over as part of the fittings when Dot and Herbert, newly married, had moved into the house, more than ten years ago.

Not that the partnership had been without its ups and downs.

'That cat should be doctored,' Dot had declared, approximately once a week, throughout the first decade of the joint ménage, and then gradually, as Minos came up towards his middle teens, the complaint had begun almost imperceptibly to change into 'That cat should be put away'. Often, Minos would rouse himself at this, and come stalking over for food, as if he had come to the conclusion that 'Put Away' must be his name. He was a resourceful cat; he had managed to live out his life under Dot's disapproving eye without (so far as one could judge by his torn ears and battle-scarred appearance) any loss of quality; and now, at nearly sixteen, he clearly had the whole thing taped, down to the last creak of the refrigerator door. Vernon and Timmie he still treated as the upstarts they were. He permitted no liberties, but now and again, on cold winter nights, he would condescend to sleep, heavy as dough, on one or other of their beds.

This was the somewhat restricted relationship which Vernon was now so desperately bewailing. Soon Timmie, who didn't like meat loaf anyway, was joining in.

'We want Minos,' they sobbed, in heart-rending unison. 'Where's Minos? Can't we go and fetch him *now*?'

The urgency of it was terrifying, coming as it did after three weeks of total indifference, during which neither of them had so much as referred to the cat's existence. In vain did Dot raise her voice above the hubbub to explain how happy Minos was with kind Mrs Timmins coming in to feed him twice a day: in vain, too, did Imogen seek to take advantage of the situation by saying loudly, 'You'll be going home, anyway, in a few days'— glancing sharply at her stepdaughter as she did so. But Dot had her can't-hear face on, and the potatoes were getting cold; and presently, what with syrup sponge for pudding, and Piggy putting her head round the door to say was all that water supposed to be dripping on to the front steps?—what with all this, the little drama died down for the time being.

It started up again, though, at bedtime, as these things do. The pleading, eager faces, rosy from a hot bath, were hard to resist, as were the pathetic, merciless little voices. It was Herbert, finally, who cracked. He came slinking guiltily down from saying goodnight to them, and announced shamefacedly, that he had promised to fetch Minos tomorrow. He'd make a detour after work, going in by car specially for the purpose.

Tomorrow? Had he gone quite crazy? How many times did Dot have to remind him that Tuesday was her Bridge afternoon, when she *had* to have the car. Did Herbert really not want her to have any social life *at all* in this place? Did he really intend to deprive her of her only pleasure in the whole week, and all for the sake of a miserable smelly old cat who ought to have been put away years ago?

'Talking of being put away years ago—' Cynthia was beginning conversationally, when a sharp little gasp from Dot stopped her in her tracks. Herbert, too, had gone quite white; but of course that might have been the Bridge party, and all that it portended for him of guilt and recrimination.

Cynthia stared from one to the other of them, bewildered, and slightly affronted.

'I was only going to ask, if anyone should come across my 1958 cheque-stubs among Ivor's things . . . I mean, they must have been put away *somewhere* all these years . . . I don't see why you all have to look so shocked!'

She pouted, and seemed about to flounce from the room; but Dot had by this time recovered herself, and hastened, with unwonted cordiality, to smooth things over. Yes, of course the cheque-stubs must be somewhere, no one would have thrown them away. She'd make a point of looking out for them . . . .

On this note of unwonted amiability the conversation came to an end. Cynthia took up her embroidery, Dot her magazine; and Imogen, looking on, wondered what on earth could be the matter. Normally, Dot and Herbert would have gone on and on for hours over such an issue as the Cat and the Bridge Party, with Herbert giving in about everything, and Dot (who could never take yes for an answer) loudly countering, point by point, all the arguments that he could have mustered in support of his point of view, if he'd still had a point of view.

As the evening went on, tranquil and unruffled, with never a cross word from anyone, Imogen grew more and more uneasy. Marital harmony was all very well, but what about the cat? Herbert had promised the children he would fetch it, and now he was going to break his promise. Well, of course he was; to expect otherwise was like expecting the butterfly to lay out the entomologist with a well-directed swipe of its gauzy wing.

It was a shame, especially with Vernon only barely recovered—if he was recovered—from last night's mysterious alarms. Perhaps this sudden fuss about Minos was an instinctive response to shock; perhaps he really did need the familiar, cross-grained old creature.

Then and there, Imogen decided to go tomorrow and fetch the cat herself. It would save a lot of argument: the children would be happy; and it wouldn't be Herbert's fault. And as for herself, a surreptitious visit to Twickenham was an idea she had been toying with for some time. A chat with Mrs Timmins, and perhaps the people next door as well, would surely provide some clues as to Dot's intentions? You can't leave people looking after your cat indefinitely, without a word about the date of your return.

*

It was strange to be getting out at Twickenham station and walking through the streets on foot, just like someone who wasn't Ivor's wife at all. Always before, she and Ivor had come by car, flashing past the neat suburban gardens, taking the quiet Sunday morning corners with an irritable squeal of tyres, just to show the world how much Ivor disliked and disapproved of this convention of family visits.

'I hate that house,' he'd say, as if this provided a solid and irrefutable excuse for exceeding the thirty-mile limit and screeching to ostentatious and insulting stops for pedestrians on crossings. 'I've always hated it, *you know* I have'—just as if the house and its inhabitants were all Imogen's fault and not his at all. And on Sunday, too, and the whole tiresome business of being a grandfather . . . why couldn't she *do* something about it, instead of just sitting there with her hair nicely back-combed?

And then, disembarking at Dot's front gate, he'd slam the car doors with punishing violence, and turn to glare balefully up at the stucco and the lace curtains.

'I was divorced from there,' he'd mutter darkly; and on this festive note would proceed, like a prisoner to the gallows, up the path towards Sunday lunch with his family.

Depressing memories were what he complained of; but of course it was boredom really. Vernon and Timmie being made to tell him how they were getting on at school, than which there was nothing he wanted to know less. Dot and Herbert in an anxious huddle, hissing to one another about how much sherry there was left. Apple pie with too many cloves, and smothered in hot yellow custard. It simply wasn't Ivor's scene.

'I have a boring daughter,' he'd once said, wonderingly, to Imogen, as if this was an aspect of his personality that he'd never really come to grips with; and Imogen hadn't quite known how to reply for the best. She'd wondered, sometimes, why he consented to come on these expeditions at all—and, indeed, why Dot continued to invite him. It must, she concluded, be some kind of reciprocal family image they were keeping up: she the devoted daughter, he the revered patriarch. Being revered is never cheap, and if, in Ivor's case, the price was sitting in front of the television waiting grimly for it to be teatime—well, in other ages it would have been some other price, and this, too, Ivor would undoubtedly have paid.

*

The winter sun struck straight into Imogen's face as she turned sharp left out of the High Street and into Dot's road. So bright it was, and so near the winter solstice, that it seemed to shine horizontally right into her eyes out of the blue, freezing sky. It dazzled her, making it hard for her to read the numbers on the gates, or to recognise one leafless lilac from another as they leaned motionless over identical gravel paths.

Thus it was that when she first saw the FOR SALE board, she quite thought she had mistaken the house. It must be No. 32, or No. 36, into which she was inadvertently turning.

But no. It was No. 34 all right. For a moment she stood staring stupidly.

'It *can't* be . . .' was her first thought; and then, 'But surely Herbert would never leave his greenfly?'

His roses, of course, really; but since it was always the greenfly that one was hearing about, it was difficult not to think of them as the central attraction. She stared again at the board.

Why? *Why?* Where were they moving to, and what for? And why hadn't they said anything to anyone? Not a word . . . not a hint . . . . Almost in a state of shock, Imogen walked slowly up the gravel path, took out the key that had been in Ivor's possession all those years, and opened the front door.

More than half the furniture was already gone. What was left was covered with dust-sheets. Even the carpets were gone, or were rolled up, stiff as mummies, against the walls, and in the silence the floorboards creaked horribly under her feet.

How *could* Dot do such a thing! And so secretive, too, so sly, without a word to anyone, not even her own children! Herbert, no doubt, had been told—must, indeed, have had his consent wrested from him for whatever it was that Dot had in mind—but it would have been the merest formality. Darling, we're emigrating to New Zealand on the 18th. That job in Wolverhampton, dear, I've just drafted your application. You see, dear, it's Vernon's catarrh we need to think about. I've told you over and over again that he needs the sea air, and now the doctor says . . . Or—here it comes!—Listen, Herbert, dear, why don't we sell up and go and live with poor Imogen? That big house . . . no mortgage to pay . . . a resident baby-sitter always on tap . . . .

The nerve of it! Imogen felt anger rising to replace the stunned bewilderment that had been her first reaction. Furiously, she stumped back down the ghostly, uncarpeted stairs, across the hall which echoed like an underground cavern to her noisy footsteps, and found herself in the kitchen.

Here, at last, in all this dead house, there were signs of habitation. Dirty crockery in the sink. A frying-pan with a fish-slice in it stood on the cooker, and beside it a kettle that still seemed slightly warm . . . and at this same moment she felt a stir of living air against her shin, a warm weight pushing, vibrating . . . Yes, it was Minos, all cupboard-love and purrs of welcome.

Just to show goodwill, she opened one of his tins of Kat-o-Meal and emptied it into his dish, though in fact it was obvious that he was getting plenty to eat. Mrs Timmins was doing well by him, that was plain. His coat, which had been looking very mangy and faded when Imogen had last seen him, was now quite glossy again, and he looked much younger than his phenomenal sixteen years. Friendly, too, and much less censorious and crotchety. In fact, after he'd finished his meal, and Imogen had made herself a cup of tea (rather to her surprise, there was fresh milk in the fridge—Mrs Timmins was certainly doing Minos proud)—after all this, the cat allowed himself to be picked up, and actually sat purring in her lap for several minutes—an honour so rare and unusual that Imogen allowed her tea to get cold rather than risk disturbing him.

He must have been really lonely, she decided, to be showing such unwonted affection, and she began to consider seriously how to get him home. He was a big, determined cat, and might spring from her arms in panic if she tried simply to carry him. A cardboard box, then? Or a basket? She decided to go across the road and discuss the problem with Mrs Timmins—who in any case must be told that she was being relieved of her charge. And Imogen would ask her, also, about this extraordinary business of selling the house. She could hardly help knowing something about it, even if Dot had attempted to keep it secret from her own family.

*

I'm sorry, Mrs Timmins is away. No, I'm sorry, I've no idea . . . No, she never said nothing about any cat, not to me she didn't. Why don't you ask them at Number 36 . . . ?

No, they didn't know anything at Number 36, either. Well, if the cat's all right, that's the main thing, isn't it? Well, why don't you leave a note, then? Whoever comes in, they can read it.

Searching for writing materials in the whitely-shrouded house was a frustrating business. Where the bureau should have been, there was now a pile of folded curtains; and in the table-drawer under the window there was nothing left but a drawing-pin and some bits of fluff.

And on top of all this, the light was already beginning to go. She must have been here quite a time, and by now the sunlight had quite gone, and the shadowy beginnings of evening were at hand. She had already tried to switch on the sitting-room light, but without avail; either the bulbs were gone, or the electricity had been turned off at the main. And it was as she stood debating all this that she became aware that the dust-sheet shrouding the settee at the far end of the room was beginning to move. Not very much—in fact, for the first moments she fancied that was a trick of the dying light; next, that it must be Minos.

But it wasn't Minos, it couldn't be, he was in the kitchen. No cat ever born or thought of could create that sudden billowing heave of whiteness, that convulsion of skidding sheets, that lurching upwards against the darkening wall . . . .

16

It was years since screams like that had been heard in this decorous road, and of course they all loved it, especially at Number 36 and at Number 32, which were nearest to the scene of the action. Along they surged, like beggars to a soup-kitchen, all agog to snatch for themselves some small share of whatever excitement it was that was going. One of the husbands, indeed, arrived armed with a poker, and, full of nostalgia for his Home Guard days, tried to organise the thing so as not to have everyone chattering, and running up and down stairs, and tripping over things.

But it was uphill work. While one party foraged for candles and matches, another succeeded in fusing what were left of the lights, and in the resultant noise and confusion a dozen burglars could have got away unnoticed. Presently, though, a degree of order was restored. Someone fetched some fuse-wire and got the lights going again, and soon the whole house had been explored from top to bottom. By the time everyone had been in and out of every room at least twice, tweaking up the dust-sheets and commenting on Dot's choice of bed-linen and furniture fabric, the thing was beginning perceptibly to pall.

No corpses. No burglars. Imogen was aware of her drop in

status. Although they were still being very sympathetic and nice to her, she knew she had become a nuisance and a disappointment.

Besides, there were dinners to cook by now, and children to be ferried to and from Brownies: what with one thing and another, they were only too glad, by six o'clock, to lend Imogen a cat-basket and get her out of the place. Their enthusiasm even ran to getting someone's nephew to drive her and Minos to the station twenty minutes too soon for the train.

They were travelling in the opposite direction from the rush-hour, and so the platform was almost deserted. The pair of them sat on a solitary bench at the far end, gusts of damp January wind whipping at them out of the darkness, piercing through the thin wickerwork to where Minos crouched, unsurprised as always, but certainly not pleased.

'Well, well! Look who's here!'

The voice, the tone of factitious surprise, were unmistakable. Imogen jerked round, clutching the cat-basket closer to her stomach, whether protectively or as a shield between herself and the newcomer, it would have been hard to say.

'Teri! What on earth are *you* doing here?'

'Waiting for the 6.48, Mrs B., just like you,' he answered equably. 'Mind if I sit here?'—and without waiting for an answer, he slid on to the bench beside her.

'Funny, running into you like this again,' he began, still on the familiar mocking note. 'Or maybe not so funny? I had a feeling you wouldn't be able to keep away from that house much longer. Bit of a risk, though, wasn't it, visiting it by daylight?'

'I don't know what you're talking about,' Imogen retorted. She found herself drawing away from him along the bench, and not only from fear. His thinness, his spots, his smell of ingrained cigarette smoke, repelled her.

'What business it is of yours I can't imagine,' she continued, 'But in fact I've been fetching my step-daughter's cat . . . .'

'A *cat* . . . ?' He gave a little yelp of startled laughter. 'So *that's* what you call it—a *cat?*' He flicked the basket lightly with his forefinger.

'Puss, puss, puss! Wotcher, puss,' he squeaked, in a contemptuous falsetto. 'Hiya, puss . . .' to which series of indignities Minos naturally made no response.

'Puss, puss . . . Hey, Mrs B., whassimatter with it? It's not moving. 'S it dead, or something?'

'He's frightened—you're frightening him—' Imogen was beginning, when Teri interrupted with another spurt of laughter.

'Come on, Mrs B., stop kidding! *I* know what you've got in there. It's what you went for, isn't it? And very sensible, if I may say so. It wouldn't be very nice, would it, Mrs B., if they discovered that the Prof, wasn't alone in the car when he crashed it? That there was a woman with him . . . a woman who jumped out just before he went into that skid?

'How did you do it, Mrs B.? Jog his elbow? Whisper a sweet nothing into his ear just when he was least expecting it? Or'— here he gave a sort of exultant cackle—'did you, Mrs B., by any chance have a *cat* with you? Do you always keep a cat handy when you're travelling, just in case . . . ? A sensible precaution, I'm sure, pity more people don't do it. But . . . a *cat* . . . !'

The joke, whatever it was, must have been exquisite, for he sat rocking with silent laughter, the bench shuddering beneath him, long after Imogen had gathered up her gloves, her cat, and her handbag, and strolled, with what she hoped was icy dignity, towards the other end of the platform. She had expected him to follow her, but when she looked back a minute later he was still there, a hunched silhouette in the darkness; surprisingly small. Then the train came in, and she lost him.

The warmth of the compartment, the somnolent faces of her fellow passengers, and the soporific rhythm of the wheels, were not conducive to clear thinking. She found her thoughts, such as they were, going round and round in the same useless circles.

Had Teri followed her to Twickenham? Or had he encountered her by chance, and decided to make the most of it? And if by chance, then what was *he* doing in Twickenham? Though of course Twickenham is a big place, people do all sorts of things in it . . . .

If he *had* followed her, then what for? To catch her out at something which would provide further 'evidence' against her, and add verisimilitude to this blackmail pantomime?

Could he actually be serious about it? Did he himself really believe these preposterous charges he'd been launching against her, up to and including this latest absurdity about her having been in the car with Ivor on the night of the accident?

And if he *didn't* believe these things, then what *was* he up to? Making the whole thing up just for the hell of it? Just for the fun of upsetting her?

It didn't upset her, of course. How could it, when it was all such complete and utter nonsense, and so easily disproved?

All the same, the mere idea that someone should *want* to upset her so much was in itself a little unnerving; and that they should be prepared to go to so much tedious and time-consuming trouble over it, too, travelling all the way to Twickenham . . . .

It all seemed so motiveless and stupid. Ignoring it had not brought it to an end; should she, then, try taking it seriously? Go to the police? That sort of thing?

'What would my dear husband have done?'—this, according to Edith, was the criterion by which a widow should make her decisions; and now, with her thoughts bumbling on in time to the train wheels, Imogen tried it out.

Faced by Teri's threats and malice, what *would* Ivor have done?

He'd have made it ten times worse, of course. He'd have loved the outrageousness of it, and would have encouraged it, at least to start with, as he always encouraged outrageousness in the young, thereby displaying his own broad-mindedness and youthful spirit. And then, when he began to get bored with the thing, or when it began to inconvenience him in some way, he'd have expected someone—most likely Imogen—to make the whole thing not have happened.

This was the trouble with nostalgic musings about Ivor, they were always barking up against this sort of thing. She felt a sudden, reluctant little surge of envy for Edith, with her endless, uncomplicated grief. Darling Desmond's posthumous advice was always so sensible, and so exactly in accordance with what Edith actually intended to do—why couldn't Ivor be like that, now that he was dead?

Imogen didn't know, of course, what sort of a husband Darling

Desmond had made when he was alive; but certainly, he made a marvellous dead one.

*

Maybe there *is* some sort of telepathy that makes one so often run into the person one has recently been thinking of? Or maybe (thought Imogen) Darling Desmond really does go sneaking around the ether, spying into people's inmost thoughts and telling tales on them, as his wife's discourse would sometimes lead one to suppose? Whatever it was, the fact remains that the first thing she saw as she toiled with Minos up the dark road towards her home, was Edith, standing in her gateway. No—in *Imogen's* gateway—silhouetted in a blaze of light from the open front door.

'Imogen!—Oh, thank goodness you're back!' she cried as soon as Imogen, hugging the cat-basket, came in sight under the street lamp. 'Oh, Imogen, my dear I've been so worried. I thought of calling the doctor, but I didn't like . . . '

Before she could finish the sentence, another figure had burst into the arc of light, its halo of fluffy hair almost ashen in the yellow glare.

'Imogen . . . Imogen . . . !' Cynthia shrieked as she stumbled forwards. 'He's back! Ivor's back! I tell you, he's *back*!'

17

There are few widows who have had vouchsafed to them one whole, clear, uninterrupted second in which to know exactly what their feelings would be if their dead husband were miraculously to return.

The utter dismay, like a black, incombustible stump right at the centre of the leaping flame of joy. The terrifying sense of inadequacy, of inability to measure up to such a moment. The blank, guilty panic at being caught out.

Not caught out *at* anything in particular. Blameless months of mourning may be all a woman has been engaged on ever since her husband's death, but all the same she knows, in that moment of truth, that she has let him down: that ever since she lost him, she has been doing something irrevocable, irreversible, to the relationship which once existed between them. Already, she is subtly unfitted to be his wife . . . four months . . . six months . . . away along a path he cannot follow. The very process of recovery is, itself, a process of destruction . . . .

At this point, mercifully, disbelief intervened, and Imogen realised that what Cynthia was saying was nonsense. Ivor was dead beyond any doubt or question; never for a moment had his identity or the fact of his death been in doubt. Cynthia must be hysterical.

As calmly as she could, Imogen led the sobbing woman indoors, sat her down at the kitchen table, and tried to get out of her what exactly had happened. Edith came in too, cried a little, and said she knew just how Cynthia was feeling—a shot in the dark if ever there was one, because so far she had no more idea than Imogen had of what had actually happened—but presumably the assertion was based on the general assumption that anything you could feel, she could feel better: she could feel anything better than you.

And in fact, her presence at this juncture *did* have a calming effect, if only because she was someone you could make tea for. It is the making of tea, not the drinking of it, that soothes nerves and gives the beverage its reputation, simply because it is all so complicated. Water exactly at the boil . . . the ceremonial warming of the pot . . . and then the soft, boring little argument about milk in first, last, or not at all . . . the proffering and refusing of sugar . . . very soon the strange, stereotyped ritual had brought Cynthia to the point where she was able to give a very-nearly coherent account of the events of the evening.

*

It had started, innocently enough, with Dot and Herbert deciding on a night out and asking Cynthia if she would baby-sit. Herbert was making amends, it seemed, for several weeks' accumulation of assorted misdemeanours, by taking his wife out to dinner; and off they had gone, in fine style, she with her beaded evening bag and long jade earrings, and he dapper and uncomfortable in his evening clothes, but pleased as Punch at having done the right thing for once.

And so from six-thirty onwards, Cynthia had been left alone. Piggy was out—sorting out her current boyfriend troubles, presumably, or maybe laying the foundations for new ones—and as for Robin, he hadn't been in all day, not so far as Cynthia was aware, anyway.

It had seemed very quiet after a while, sitting there all by herself doing her embroidery, with the boys sound asleep upstairs, and nothing good on television: and so, after a while—nine o'clock, was it, or maybe a little later?—she had grown restless, and decided to look around the house and make sure that everything was all right.

All right? Why shouldn't it be all right?—and at this Cynthia bridled a little, and pointed out that after all she *had* been left in charge. And no—No, she hadn't felt scared, not at that stage. She'd just felt *restless*, for Heaven's sake, couldn't they understand? Which of course Edith at once proceeded to do, with many a little nod of the head, and a tentative sniff or two just in case it turned out to be something to do with the family bereavement.

Mollified by these small tributes to sensitivity in general and to her own in particular, Cynthia resumed her story.

Feeling restless, as just established, she had naturally enough found herself, after a while, wandering into poor Ivor's study and idly opening the drawers of his desk, one after another.

Searching for something? No, of course not. Looking through his papers? What an idea! Just thumbing through them idly, for Heaven's sake, just for something to *do*: couldn't they *understand*?—and once again Edith, like a soldier leaping to attention, instantly did so.

Imogen wasn't quite so quick; and her insensitive curiosity rapidly brought Cynthia up against some kind of a block, and she was unable to go on.

She'd come across some letter? Some document that had upset her? With this business of idly thumbing through some-one else's private papers, you can never tell, can you?

But no . . . no . . . . She kept shaking her head at all these suggestions; and then, rather disturbingly, she was seen once more to be crying—a kind of helpless, watery sobbing, with the lamplight glistening on her wet cheeks and on her pale froth of hair. It was no use going on at her like this, she sobbed, she just couldn't bear it . . . couldn't bear to talk about it. It had been such a shock, you see; and it would be even more of a shock for Imogen: she wished she'd never said a thing about it, she wished she'd kept it to herself.

'And it's not even as if I *believe* in ghosts,' she burst out, feebly indignant. 'I've never even been to one of those meetings where they . . .'

'Of course you haven't. As if you would . . .' Edith was all over her now, patting, hand-squeezing, stroking in a way that Imogen (shoddy, inadequate mourner that she was) had never allowed. 'Of course you haven't, dear, and of course you don't believe in ghosts, neither do I; that would be blasphemy, and Spiritualism, and that sort of thing. But we do know, don't we, dear, that our dear ones haven't really left us. They are still here, watching over us day and night . . . . Darling Desmond, and dear Ivor too; right now they're . . .'

Cynthia's screams rang terrifyingly through the quiet room. They echoed up and down and back and forth in the large empty house—it was a miracle, Imogen thought afterwards, that the boys hadn't been awakened—scream after scream, beyond all human control: she seemed to be in a veritable paroxysm of terror.

'Hysterics,' diagnosed Imogen, shakily. 'Water, Edith. Cold water . . .' and Edith, pausing only long enough to say, with a touch of triumph, 'You see?—I *knew* I should have called the doctor' (just as if anyone had stopped her), hastened to the tap.

With wet flannels, soothing words, and brandy, they managed at last to quieten the panic-stricken woman; bit by bit the screams were replaced by broken, exhausted sobbing.

'I—I'm sorry—' Cynthia managed to gasp once or twice; and 'It was silly of me . . . I didn't mean . . .'

She was still trembling, and clutching both of Edith's hands for support, and Edith, in her element at last, took command of the situation, and led the distracted victim gently, and with murmured words of consolation, up the stairs to her room. Imogen felt, for once, truly grateful to her next-door-neighbour. Edith could be a very real comforter of sorrow, she now realised, if only one had the knack of sorrowing in the right way.

Meantime, as became her inferior aptitude for this kind of scene, Imogen applied herself to the ancillary services of grief— hot-water-bottles; extra blankets; unearthing Cynthia's pale-green tranquillisers from under the table-mats in the sideboard; phoning the doctor—

Or not phoning the doctor? Was Cynthia ill, or had she really come upon something terrible in Ivor's desk? If the latter, then a doctor would merely be a further complication . . . .

Leaving the kettles on a low gas, Imogen tiptoed across the hall—tiptoed, because she was supposed to be engaged on a work of mercy, not of investigation, and Edith's ears were very acute for this kind of thing.

The study door was wide open, just as Cynthia must have left it when she fled, and the light was on. The desk drawers, on the other hand, were all neatly shut, without even a corner of paper protruding. Presumably, Cynthia had slammed the drawer shut on whatever it was she had seen . . . almost as if it might be going to spring out at her . . . ?

*

Income-tax forms. Circulars about the new rating-system. More income-tax . . . . Imogen moved on to the next drawer, and the next.

Receipts. Bills. University business. It was only when she came to the bottom drawer of all that she became aware that her hands were trembling, and that she was in the grip of a terrible feeling of reluctance to go on. Afterwards, she wondered if it had been some kind of a premonition; but of course it wasn't. It was just that whatever it was that had frightened Cynthia *must* be in this drawer, simply because it wasn't in any of the others. This was the last one.

Gingerly, Imogen gave a half-hearted little tweak to the handles; but of course the drawer didn't budge. She pulled harder . . . harder . . . it was heavier than she remembered. Then, with sudden, noisy defiance, she put forth all her strength and yanked it wide open.

*

The thing stared her in the face: just as it must have stared Cynthia in the face when, already guilty and on edge from her illicit prying, she'd furtively peeped into this last drawer of all.

'PLEASE LEAVE MY THINGS ALONE' it said, in Ivor's bold, unmistakable handwriting.

*

That such a notice should still exist was not, of course, so very extraordinary—though how it could have got into this drawer, on top of all the other papers, was still a puzzle. And you could well imagine the effect it must have had upon Cynthia, coming upon it unawares, and being less familiar (presumably) than Imogen with Ivor's habit of writing just this kind of notice whenever his work happened to have put him in a bad mood. Maybe he hadn't done it in Cynthia's day; but certainly ever since Imogen had been married to him, such a notice as this lying on top of his papers had been virtually a message telling her that the work in question wasn't going too well. She understood very well that these peremptory and superfluous orders to the world at large (because no

one would ever have dared to touch any of his papers anyway)
gave him a compensatory feeling of power, and also the vague
feeling that the obstacles he was encountering had somehow
been someone else's fault.

All this hard-won understanding was useless now. Obso-
lete. Finished. It would never be needed again. Staring down
at the familiar, sharply-worded missive, Imogen ached with
longing for those fits of truculent ill-humour, of unreasonable accusations, that she alone knew how to soothe. Blinking
back the tears, she picked up the paper, and held it under the
light.

*

She blinked again. She stared, and felt bewilderment growing
monstrous within her. Her brain was maybe a little slow in
grasping the significance of what she saw, but already her stomach knew. She felt it contract; and she felt the hair on the back
of her neck rising.

The paper in her hand was new paper, not paper four
months old. The writing on it was new writing—written today
or yesterday, not last summer. The ink was bright and fresh, it
couldn't—not possibly—be four months old or more.

*

You can't be sure, she told herself. You need proof.

You shall have proof. There, lying on the desk, was the
writing-pad she'd bought herself only yesterday. It was open,

the top sheet had been ripped hastily off, leaving a narrow, ragged triangle of paper still adhering to the binding. That slanting, uneven edge of paper would exactly fit—wouldn't it—against the slanting, uneven edge of the 'please leave my things alone' notice that she still clutched between finger and thumb.

Or would it?

Only one way not to find out, and that was not to try. Not to lay those two torn edges alongside one another, like bits of a jigsaw . . . *not* to find out if they exactly fitted. At the moment, they only *looked* as if they did.

It was easy, really. Couldn't be easier. All she had to do was to throw away this sheet of paper just as she had thrown away that whisky bottle, washed up that glass, and put that Lexicon back on the shelf.

*

The embers of the dining-room fire would still be red, if she carried the thing in there right now, and poked it deep, deep in among the dying coals. She could stand there and watch the brief flame leaping, living out its tiny life-span, and then harmlessly dying.

It would be over. The whole thing wouldn't have happened.

That had often been the job of Ivor's wife—to make things not have happened. She would merely be doing it once more—for one last time.

*

The two edges fitted exactly. For a moment, she stood numbly, marvelling at the perfection of it, as if it was the work of some fabulous master-craftsman.

Then, like Cynthia, she began to scream.

18

By the time Dot and Herbert arrived home, well after midnight, the moments of high drama were over. Cynthia, knocked unconscious by two of Edith's blue sleeping-pills on top of several of her own pale-green tranquillisers—not to mention the brandy—lay now like the dead. Darling Desmond's putative attitude to the situation (surely one not quite up his street?) had been gone through exhaustively, and the other-worldly revelations he came up with (that what must be must be, and that these things are sent to try us) had been given due weight. Imogen's thoughts were now revolving round more practical possibilities: like who had been forging Ivor's handwriting, and why?

Because forgery, of course, must be the explanation.

She was ashamed, now, of having screamed. For one thing, it put her into a category wherein Edith's ministrations became unavoidable: and for another, she hated the feeling of having lost her head and made a fool of herself.

After the first, unreasoning panic was over, she'd gone back to the study, and had examined the drawer carefully, looking for clues. The first thing she'd noticed was that the mysterious Minoan manuscript, whose scattered pages she'd gathered together yesterday into a loose pile and laid on the desk, was now neatly sorted into chapters, each clipped together with a paper-clip, and the whole secured by an elastic band. There was more of it than she'd realised at first, it made quite a solid little pile of paper lying there in the drawer; but it still wasn't of book length—her experienced eye told her this at once.

Five chapters, that was all. Probably about a third of what had been originally intended. Curious to assess the point at which the young, long-ago Ivor had given up, she began leafing through the last few pages—and straight away got another shock, almost as great as the shock of finding the warning notice.

Since yesterday morning, alterations had been made. With a modern, blue-black biro, words had been crossed out, corrections added—intelligent corrections, so far as Imogen could judge:

'Around 1700 b.c.' had been crossed out, and 'Between 1550 b.c. and 1400 b.c.' written-in over the top, the new, fresh ink standing out like dark silk against the yellowing pages. Her heart beating strangely, she turned the next page, and the next, until she came to the last one of all.

She stared. She could not believe it.

Someone was going on with the book. Since this morning, two new paragraphs had been added. Her eyes scanned incredulously the bold, familiar writing.

It seemed to be the resumption of some earlier discussion of the Cretan scripts and their decipherment; and it started off, so far as Imogen could judge, in a perfectly coherent and scholarly way. After a few sample lines of the curious, angular script (which by now was becoming almost familiar to Imogen), the text continued:

'The clue, of course, lies in the inflexional character of the language. Imagine yourself for a moment to be living in a new Dark Age, where Latin has been utterly forgotten. You are trying to decipher one of these unknown master-pieces—and the first thing you will notice is that while the words are just as varied as you would expect, the endings of the words are *not*. The signs "i" and "is" and "orum" and so on recur over and over again as word-endings. You will thus conclude damn, damn, damn, all this is perfectly useless, I'm too late, it's all *in* Ventris, what on earth is the point of going on? Why did I ever come back into the world of the living? Everything moves too fast, I can't keep up, I'm used to the other world now, where things go slowly as in a dream.

But if I *had* to come back into the land of the living, why didn't they at least let me come back sooner? I've been dead too long, my brain has begun to rot, I can't think any more.'

By now, Imogen's hand was shaking so much that she could scarcely hold the page.

A joke, she kept saying to herself. A cruel, ridiculous joke. Don't look for sense in it, don't keep reading it over and over, there won't *be* any sense, why should there be? It's only a joke, a stupid, horrible joke.

But perpetrated by whom?

Robin? Teri? These were the names that sprang naturally to mind when something outrageous was afoot; but this time it wouldn't do. Whoever it was who had sunk to this level of tasteless spite had gone to immense trouble over it—weeks and months of gruelling practice must have gone into the achieving of so brilliant and accomplished a forgery. It was impossible to suppose that either Robin or Teri were capable of this sort of application—Robin, who got bored with everything within minutes, or Teri, who didn't even know the word 'blackmail'.

Whoever had forged the writing—and indeed the style—so perfectly was someone of very different calibre.

It was the ease of the thing that was so amazing. Imogen was no graphologist, but common-sense told her that deliberately forged writing, even if superbly executed, would surely bear traces of artificiality, of laboured, over-meticulous penmanship.

She bent closer to the page, holding it once more under the lamp.

Not a sign, not a suspicion, of the kind of awkwardness she was looking for. The writing ran boldly, effortlessly—sometimes even carelessly—across the page, as though the writer, whoever he was, had practised and perfected the imitation for so long that it came to him as naturally as breathing.

What other possibilities were there? Was she, perhaps, in her over-wrought state, imagining a greater degree of resemblance than was really there?

Sitting down at the desk, Imogen spread the papers before her, and set herself, quite systematically, to search for flaws in the imitation: laying the new paragraphs alongside assorted old ones, and comparing them letter by letter, and, wherever possible, word by word.

The two sets of writing were identical.

What in the world was going on? Was there someone who, for some unimaginable motive, was trying to make her believe, in the teeth of all the known and incontrovertible facts, that her husband was still alive? Or was it some mad spiritualist, trying to convince her that Ivor's spirit still hovered around its old haunts, poking its supernatural nose into things, interfering with perfectly sensible earthly arrangements, and generally keeping its loved ones on their toes?

Just like Darling Desmond. And hot on the heels of this thought came another, unheralded and unbidden: Ivor would have loved it to be like that. He'd have loved to be a ghost, to amaze and startle, as only a ghost can; to appear and disappear at will, entirely at his own other-worldly convenience; to retain, though dead, a finger in every pie, a say in every family decision, and at the same time to enjoy his four-dimensional option of disappearing in a puff of smoke whenever anything became troublesome.

'One foot in the grave and the other in the rat-race'—that's how he'd have described it, and he would have exploited it for all it was worth, getting the best out of both worlds and then vanishing with a gleeful rattle of chains just before the trouble started.

Soon, he would be famous. 'Dead Professor Walks Again' would be the headline; and there would be meetings of the Psychical Research Society to discuss his authenticity.

The Barnicott Ghost: it would be a household word, in all the local guide-books, a tourist attraction. Sooner or later a teenage blonde would get mixed up in the thing, and her picture would be in all the Sunday papers alongside his. A book might even be written about him.

And then television, of course. Did ghosts ever appear on television?—Ivor's ghost would. She could just hear his mellow, disembodied voice putting the interviewer right on some bit of supernatural know-how . . . .

For a moment, she fancied she really *could* just hear it: 'Imogen, for God's sake, why can't you . . . ?' but of course it was her imagination.

*

From now on, she must expect to imagine this sort of thing; for, of course, the affair was going to escalate. Whether it was fraud or spirit-messages, they weren't going to leave it at this.

Come to think of it, it had escalated already—had, in fact, been escalating all the time. 'You've got a poltergeist,' Cynthia had declared, and from that moment on the sequence of events had been exactly what one might have expected if her hypothesis had been correct. Objects mysteriously out of place; minor, mischievous damage; and invariably one or other of the children involved. In poltergeist phenomena there was always a child involved—so Imogen had read; and no doubt the perpetrator of the trick had read up the subject likewise.

There had already been one Manifestation—the face floating above Vernon's bed. Soon, there would be others.

Thank God it was only a trick.

Imogen felt a pang of guilt at this so summarily depriving Ivor of his after-life and all its attendant fun and games; especially as he had worked so hard to attain it.

Well, he must have done. She pictured how it must have been for his bewildered, recalcitrant spirit during these past four months. Fluttering and feeble it would have been at first, from the great shock of death—and no doubt looking vainly around for her, Imogen, to do something about it.

And she had done nothing. Well, what *could* she have done?

'And I sprinkled white meal over the strengthless dead . . .
I made sacrifice . . . and many ghosts flocked together to drink the black blood and to gain strength there from . . . .'

*

'Good God! Are you asleep, or something?'

Dot's voice, fresh and strident from her evening's outing, burst across Imogen's consciousness, driving the disjointed quotation (from somewhere or other in Homer, wasn't it?) right out of her mind. She blinked at Dot stupidly; then straightened up, realising that she had been slumped forward over the desk, more than half asleep, her elbows among the papers.

'What *are* you doing?' continued Dot; and then, without waiting for an answer, she launched into the story of her own evening.

It had been an exciting one, by hers and Herbert's standards. They had danced as well as dined; they had seen a drug-addict leaning against some railings; and they had stood up (or rather Dot had stood Herbert up) to the taxi-driver who'd tried to charge them double because it was after midnight.

He'd succeeded, actually; but (to judge by her own account) she'd got in a lot of satisfying ripostes first, and so victory, of a sort, had been enjoyed by all. Oh, and they'd seen someone walking down the Parade carrying a nursery fire-guard. At *this* time of night! Whoever would be wanting to carry a . . .

It seemed a shame, really, to break in on such blissful reminiscences, but it had to be done. It was just possible that Dot might be able to shed some light on the mysterious happenings of this evening; and there was, in any case, the furtive selling of the house in Twickenham to be explained. While Imogen was debating in her mind which of these two uncomfortable topics to raise first, the decision was summarily taken out of her hands. Dot broke off in mid-sentence and pointed like a gun-dog:

'*What's that cat doing here?*' she demanded: and for the first time since she'd entered the house, Imogen recollected the existence of Minos. How he'd got out of his basket (or got someone to get him out) she would never know—cats are like that—but anyway, here he was now, curled up fast asleep on the seat of Ivor's big leather chair.

'Well—' she was beginning apologetically, and then, suddenly, What the hell? she thought, and moved over to the attack. After all, the selling of a house surely demands more explanations than the fetching of a cat?

*

Dot was almost aggressively off-hand. It was a good time to sell, she pointed out, the agent had said so. He had, apparently, complimented her, Dot, on the singular goodness of the time, and also on her foresight in having installed central heating in spite of the fact that Herbert enjoyed sawing up logs on Saturday afternoons. The exercise was good for him, he'd pleaded; and, 'What about your fibrositis?' she'd countered, quick as a flash. And now, hey presto, she'd been proved right, to the tune of an extra £750 on the selling price, and if that didn't cure Herbert's fibrositis, nothing would.

And yes, well, she was sorry she hadn't told Imogen about all these plans, but she hadn't wanted to worry her (people never do want to worry you about issues over which you might oppose them, Imogen reflected); and besides, the house hadn't been sold yet, had it, so there wasn't, actually, anything to tell. Where were they moving to? Well, Dot had never believed in crossing bridges until she came to them; and all Imogen's efforts to convince her that she *had* come to this one, right here in her stepmother's home, evoked only the blank, unhearing look with which Dot habitually countered arguments which fell outside her chosen area of conflict.

Imogen had earlier decided not to tell Dot about the mysterious up-heaving of the dust-sheet until tomorrow, not wanting to upset her last thing at night; but now she changed her mind, and decided that Dot could do with all the upsetting she could get. Determined to wipe that vacant, impervious look off her step-daughter's face if it was the last thing she did, Imogen launched straight into her story, making it as melodramatic and unnerving as she knew how. So successful was she that Herbert gave a little 'Oh!' of dismay and scurried from the room, while Edith— who was still hanging around in hopes of further morsels of disaster—gasped, and dabbed at her eyes with her handkerchief. Though how such a narrative could have reminded her in any way of Darling Desmond, it was hard to imagine.

Only Dot seemed unperturbed.

Squatters, she asserted. Everyone has squatters these days (she made it sound like a new hair-style) if they leave their house unoccupied. And anyway, it was the agent's business, not hers. Imogen could ring him up if she liked, his number was, what was it? She'd got it upstairs, somewhere. And talking of upstairs, she, Dot, would like to go up to bed now, if Imogen didn't very much mind, she'd had a long day.

Even for Dot in her can't-hear mood, this was taking imperturbability a bit far. Imogen watched, puzzled, as her stepdaughter made her exit, yawning excessively, as though to say, See if you can make me care!

But later on, as she passed their door on her way to bed, Imogen heard a sound that reassured her a little. Dot and Herbert were quarrelling. This indication that Dot had reverted to her normal self filled Imogen with relief.

*

You couldn't call it eavesdropping, exactly, not when they were talking so loudly. Besides, wasn't it Imogen's right—indeed her duty—to know what was going on in her own house? They might be talking about the mysterious writing in Ivor's desk: that Herbert had done it, or something.

It wasn't like listening at the keyhole. All she was doing was sitting on the stairs. And anyway, no one could possibly catch her at it, they'd all gone to bed long ago.

Her conscience finally set at rest by this last consideration, Imogen leaned forward, her forehead pressed against the banisters, trying to tune-in to the mumble and staccato of voices going on behind the closed door. Rather to her surprise, it was Herbert whom she could hear most clearly.

'I did *not* give her the key,' he was protesting with unusual vigour, 'I didn't even know she was back. And anyway, I haven't *got* a key . . . .'

Poor Herbert. Always weakening his case by throwing in a second reason after the first, like throwing a pike in after a goldfish. I haven't *got* a key . . . . Dot would soon make mincemeat of *that* one.

She did. What about Mrs Timmins' key? And the key at No 36? And the one with the house-agents? And the one that had always been kept under the brick by the back door . . . .

Such a jangling plethora of keys . . . . Herbert must have found the clink of them terrifying, but he went gamely on:

'I didn't! I tell you I didn't . . .'

If only he could have stopped there—but on he went, like a lemming to its doom: '. . . and even if I had, it couldn't have been on a Tuesday, because . . .'

Game, set and match to Dot. It was annoying the way Dot always let her voice drop as soon as victory was assured, but Imogen could still make out quite a bit of it: to the effect that *some* men consider their wives' feelings now and again, and that if Herbert was as sorry as all that for the wretched woman, then why didn't he something something something and be done with it?

It was annoying not to be able to hear the crucial words, but Imogen felt in no doubt as to the gist of it.

That Woman. Herbert must have been seeing her again. Or promising that he wouldn't, and then leaving around a picture-postcard of Cheltenham Town Hall which ended up 'Till Friday—Take care of yourself', or some such inflammatory message.

Friday? Friday? No, it was *Tuesday* they were fighting about this time. *This* Tuesday. Today, in fact—or yesterday, rather, it being already long after midnight.

'I tell you I *don't* know, I wasn't *there*,' Herbert was affirming desperately. 'And if I had been, I'd never have *something something something*! Have a heart, Dot, how can *I* help it if she takes it into her head to . . .'

*

Not very gallant; but then what lover is, when driven into a corner by his wife? By now, Imogen could hardly suppress her giggles as she pictured Herbert and his lady whipping that dust-sheet over themselves when they heard the unexpected sound of Imogen's key in the door; and then lying there, growing more and more restive and uneasy, while Imogen explored the house at her leisure, made herself tea, talked to the cat . . . . Just like Herbert to choose, as the moment for their getaway, that very moment when Imogen had come back into the room; and getting himself hopelessly entangled in the dust-sheet in the process.

Or maybe it was his lady-love? Maybe it was a beautifully

shared ineptitude that had brought them together in the first place? Two ineffectual hearts beating as one . . . it was touching, really, and on this occasion it would seem that luck had been on their side. While Imogen ran screaming to the neighbours, imagining goodness knows what of murder and mayhem, Herbert and That Woman could easily have slipped out into the street and got away unnoticed. They could even have slammed the front door, tripped over the scraper, and paused to exchange a few honeyed words about whose idea it had all been in the first place, and still they'd have got away with it.

After all her terror that afternoon—to have the whole thing ending in farce.

Maybe all the rest of the mysteries would turn out to be farce, too. Maybe by tomorrow they'd all be laughing their heads off. Ha ha! Ho ho! Would you credit it . . . ?

*

And it was only after she was in bed, and on the very verge of falling asleep, that it occurred to Imogen that it couldn't possibly have been Herbert at the Twickenham house between four-thirty and five yesterday afternoon. According to Cynthia (who knew, because she'd been baby-sitting) he and Dot had left here, all dressed up for the evening, before six-thirty. He must have arrived home, then, by six at the latest.

It couldn't be done, all the way from Twickenham.

And it didn't occur to her, drowsy as she by then was, that Dot, too, must have known that it couldn't be done.

19

'Well, what about Robin, then?' Dot suggested. 'After all, he *is* his son. You *can* inherit handwriting, can't you?'

What a futile suggestion. They all knew Robin's handwriting—cramped and reluctant, and as different from his father's as it could well be. Robin hated writing, particularly letters, and it showed.

'Well, Cynthia then,' Dot went on, doggedly unhelpful, '*She* might . . . Oh no, though. Those airmail letters . . . all thin and pointed . . . No.'

Dot, it seemed to Imogen, was being singularly useless in this crisis—indeed, she seemed to lack all sense of it *being* a crisis, standing there in the doorway, arms resignedly folded, as though helping Imogen with clues in a crossword puzzle. When, immediately after breakfast, Imogen had asked her to come along to the study and give some advice, she had come reluctantly: and once there, had stared at the pages Imogen tremulously held out to her with a sort of wooden incomprehension.

'No,' she had said at last: 'No . . .'—though whether it was the facts in front of her that she was rejecting, or Imogen's obvious intention of bothering her with them, was not made clear.

Pressed for further comment, she had allowed, grudgingly, that the handwriting was 'rather like' her father's: adding, as a rider, that 'Millions of people have the same handwriting'.

'Just like they have the same Christian names,' she finished triumphantly, brandishing the false analogy like a rabbit out of a hat. And on Imogen's suggesting, mildly, that in the case of handwriting, 'millions' was surely an overstatement, she had merely shrugged, and pointed out that Well, it must be *someone*.

A deduction that couldn't be faulted; and so, her ruffled ego soothed by having thus scored an incontrovertible point in logic, she condescended to join Imogen for a few minutes more of futile speculation. Indeed, after a bit, the thing clearly began to get a hold on her, for the names of Robin and Cynthia proved to be only the first on a list of ever-mounting improbability and randomness.

Indeed, it seemed to Imogen that her step-daughter was treating the whole thing as if it was a game, and not even a game of skill; and so, as tactfully as she knew how, she attempted to narrow the field a little. The forger must, for example, be someone who had at least been acquainted with Ivor; and who had, right now, access to the house by night and by day.

'I suppose you mean *I* did it,' said Dot, aggrieved; but she could not sulk for long, because almost at once she had an inspiration: a very sudden and intriguing one, to all appearances.

'Myrtle!' she exclaimed. 'What about Myrtle? You know, that friend of yours with the earrings. The one who—'

Who was Ivor's mistress during that summer of '69. Imogen could understand why Dot's voice had faltered in embarrassment; but in fact she herself had never felt any great resentment

over the affair. Ivor's mistresses had always been less important to him than his reviews and his television appearances,
and Imogen had always understood this perfectly well: it was
the mistresses who were put out by it. It wasn't that he didn't
enjoy love, he did; but he enjoyed praise even more, and incidentally found that it demanded far less in return. This had been
Myrtle's trouble all along, she hadn't understood the kind of
competition she was up against: and so she had come a cropper,
just like the rest of them.

Still, it was all a long time ago now, and there were no hard
feelings. Myrtle and Imogen had managed to remain quite good
friends—indeed, was it not Myrtle who had been the first of all
her acquaintances to summon up the courage to invite her to a
party after Ivor's death? And incidentally, to introduce her to the
awful Teri; but you couldn't in fairness blame her for that.

'Myrtle?—Oh no, not *Myrtle*,' she said aloud. No need to
increase Dot's embarrassment by labouring the point right
now, but in fact Imogen had come to know Myrtle's handwriting very well indeed during that summer, when letters had
arrived for Ivor by every post, full of yearning and passion.
He'd loved it, Imogen remembered, except for the bother of
answering them.

'Well, then, what about . . . ?' Dot was resuming, tireless as
an armoured tank; but at just this moment Robin strolled into
the room.

It was unusual to see Robin up and about by nine-forty-five
in the morning, but Imogen checked her instinctive reaction of
surprise, and began explaining to him, right from the beginning,
the mystery she had stumbled upon last night in Ivor's desk.

Robin listened, apparently with attention, until she had finished. Then he picked up a page of the manuscript and held it alongside the 'Please leave my things alone' note. He examined the latter with especial care.

'Why don't you answer it?' he enquired at last, dropping it back on to the desk: 'Dear Spook: With reference to yours of the 16th, we would like to inform you that your request will be receiving our early attention, and in the meantime why the hell can't you leave *us* alone?—Signed, Imogen, Robin, Dot, and—'

'Not me! . . . Don't include me . . . !'

Dot clapped her hand over her mouth, as if suddenly conscious of the idiocy of her exclamation. Robin smiled drily.

'Bit slow on the uptake this morning, aren't we, dear?' he enquired of his sister pityingly.

Imogen did not bother to listen to her retort, or to the boring brother-and-sister wrangling which was bound to follow. They were being useless, both of them: tiresomely and deliberately useless; but suddenly it didn't matter any more, because she knew, now, what she was going to do. Do entirely by herself, with no need of help or co-operation from either of them.

She should have done it several nights ago, really; but better late than never.

*

It was cold here, behind the floor-length study curtains; colder than she'd imagined it would be, for inside the room the fire still glowed red: in the midnight quiet she could hear, now and then, the soft fall of the coals. But here, in her chosen

171

hiding-place, the heat did not penetrate. The heavy curtains, chosen specially to keep the draught from Ivor as he worked far into the night, and often into the beginnings of dawn, formed now a total barrier between herself and the warmed room; while behind her were the french windows: nothing but a black, icy expanse of glass between herself and the freezing garden.

She'd been standing here, flattened against the glass, for more than an hour now. She'd heard the clock in the hall strike one, and then two; and still no one had come.

She'd made things as easy as she could for them—even tempting. The manuscript open at the right page; pens, pencils, fresh paper all to hand. The front door she'd left unbolted, and slightly ajar, while the study door itself was invitingly half-open, just revealing the faint glow of the dying fire. Never can marauder have encountered so nearly-loving a reception.

Who would it be? Acquaintance? Friend? Close member of the family?

Which was the area of her life which, after tonight's revelations, would never be the same again?

She could feel her mind revolving now, faster and faster, into some kind of half-dream. She pictured first Teri, mincing into the room, skinny and black as a winter twig against the glow of the dying fire. Then Dot, mountainous, larger than life in some kind of spreading cloak. She was laughing, as in real life Dot hardly ever laughed . . . and then, suddenly, Imogen was wide awake again: tensely, quiveringly awake.

For someone *was* coming. Footsteps, soft as dropped plasticine, were moving across the hall . . . pausing . . . lapsing into silence as they reached the open doorway.

A sultry, ominous silence. It was like thunder-clouds gathering in your ears.

Perhaps it had been a mistake to leave the door so invitingly open? Perhaps it had put the visitor on his guard: what are they up to?—why haven't they shut it as usual?—how can I feel right if I don't start by turning the door-knob gently, gently, in the way at which I have become so skilled . . . ?

Imogen was intensely, piercingly aware of the unseen eye that must be peering now through the crack of the door, just as her own eye was peering through the crack in the curtains: two glances that must never meet and yet shared an intense, unspeakable intimacy as they scanned precisely the same cosy, treacherous scene of firelight and old, well-loved books . . . .

Well, not precisely the same. Ivor's big leather armchair would be outside the intruder's field of vision as yet; as also would be the papers, laid out so invitingly, like a flytrap, on the old polished mahogany of the desk. Moreover, the eye at the crack of the door doesn't know, yet, about its counterpart behind the curtain. It doesn't know that it is being spied on. All *it* is doing is seeking for general assurance that the room is empty. Compared with this other eye, behind the curtain, it is innocent.

Dark as a tree, the thing came round the door.

Except that trees don't. The huge, headless thing had moved half way across the room before Imogen took in that from the base of the trunk peeped human feet, bare, and pinkly gleaming in the firelight. And it wasn't headless at all . . . nor even huge . . . quite ordinary in fact, for what she had taken for chest and shoulders was now flung off—a hood merely, loose and dark—revealing—as in any fairy-story—a beautiful girl. The golden

173

hair swung to her waist, and the shadowed curve of the soft cheek took on an unearthly loveliness as she moved into the ambience of the dying fire.

In fact, what with one thing and another, Piggy was hard to recognise. With her hair loose like this . . . with her usual sullen, wary expression replaced by this look of rapt, incredulous wonder . . . with the silly, pretentious burnous in the near-darkness swaying like a magic cloak around her—Imogen stared, incredulous, as the girl moved, with incomparable slow grace, towards the centre of the room: towards the big leather chair which had always been Ivor's.

*

Imogen did not need to peer through the crack between the curtains any more: did not need actually to *see* the girl sinking on her knees, burying her face in the old, worn leather, and drinking in its nostalgic scent as if it was oxygen and she on the point of death. Nor did Imogen need to hear—indeed, she stopped her ears in order *not* to hear—the endearments, the soft, wild pleadings into the empty night:

'Come back, my love! Come back! I'm here, I'm waiting . . . !'

20

'Well, that explains *everything*!' declared Cynthia. 'In love with Ivor! Would you believe it! No wonder we couldn't get any sense out of her about her "boyfriend trouble". Though mind you, Imogen, I suspected something of the sort all along . . . .'

'I'm sure you did,' said Imogen drily—and then repented almost at once of her sarcasm. Cynthia had a habit of being wiser, after a greater variety of events, than almost anyone Imogen had ever known, but this was no time to start an argument about it. Cynthia had, after all, suffered quite a bad attack of nerves last night, and this morning—as is so often the privilege of the one who has caused all the trouble—was having breakfast in bed. In her pink lacy bedjacket, and with her fluff of pale hair all anyhow, she looked like a bruised child. The blue eyes, still muzzy from all those sleeping-pills and things, looked up at Imogen questioningly.

'Have another piece of toast?' Imogen invited, trying to make amends—though in fact no such effort was necessary. Cynthia was more or less impervious to sarcasm (perhaps this was one of the things that had made her so difficult to divorce?), and had taken Imogen's snide remark as a compliment.

'Yes, well, I've always had this sort of rapport thing with the young,' she agreed modestly. 'As Teddy always used to say— Oh, thank you—Yes; yes please . . . Thanks a lot . . . .'

To avert being told who Teddy was and what he used to say, Imogen was feverishly plying her companion with butter, marmalade, more coffee . . . and sure enough, it worked. Cynthia's stream-of-consciousness soon meandered obediently back to the matter in hand: namely, Piggy, and Imogen's strange encounter with her last night. The last half of the story was even more dramatic than the first, and Cynthia was soon listening open-mouthed, asking pertinent questions here and there, and putting Imogen right on points of detail.

Not that Cynthia had actually been present, of course, or knew anything about the sequence of events, but she was very quick at knowing what *should* have happened.

'But she was still crying, Imogen, she must have been . . .'

'Oh, but Imogen, she'd never have said a thing like *that*, not at such a moment . . . .' 'Oh, but she couldn't have, Imogen, not unless the light was on . . . .'

And so on and so on. Imogen began to wish that she didn't have to tell the story at all, and particularly not to Cynthia. She would have preferred, for Piggy's sake as well as her own, to have kept the whole thing to herself and never mentioned it to anyone: but the way it had all ended made secrecy impossible.

*

She had grown stiff, standing there behind the curtain. Stiff and cold, and aching in all her limbs. Once or twice, she had imagined that Piggy must have tiptoed away, but each time, when she peeped through the curtains, the girl was still there, spreadeagled across the chair in an attitude of silent, abandoned grief. She was no longer weeping, but neither was she asleep. Her eyes were bright, and wide open, staring, apparently, straight into Imogen's own eye, though of course they couldn't have been. In the faint light from the dying fire it was impossible to read their expression, they looked like two silver beads; the rest of the girl's face was quite lost in the shadows.

More than once, as the aching of her back worsened, Imogen was tempted to throw in her hand; to walk out from behind the curtain and make a clean breast of it. Yes, I'm sorry, I *was* spying; but not on *you* . . . I never meant . . . I'd never have dreamed . . . I was expecting something quite absolutely different . . . .

Piggy's anger she could have faced. It was the girl's embarrassment that would be so insupportable. How awful for the poor child to learn that her most private emotions had been spied on, the extravagant secrets of her heart laid bare. For someone so young, and so emotional, it could be quite traumatic.

No. Backache or no backache, she must stick it out.

Hardly had this heroic decision crystallised in her mind, than she became aware that it was unnecessary. Her vigil was right now coming to an end. The figure on the chair was moving.

Imogen dared not peep through the crack any more. Flattening herself against the glass, holding her breath in sheer relief, she waited to hear the soft barefoot padding towards the door . . . the swish of the burnous as it brushed the lintel . . . and then the lovely, luxurious silence that would swing back into the room once the girl was well and truly gone.

That all this wasn't happening was at first unclear. Through the muffling folds of curtain, the direction and quality of the sounds were hard to assess, and Imogen only took in what was happening when the long, heavy curtain swept softly against her, and Piggy stepped through into the moonlight.

Even then, Imogen might have escaped unnoticed. She was still partially hidden, and Piggy, her hair all around her in a silver waterfall, looking neither to the right nor to the left, stood as one enchanted, her eyes upraised towards the moon, which hung, larger than life it seemed, and almost exactly at the full, just above the bare, motionless elms. Their black shadows lay across the frost-bitten lawn at a strange angle, never seen at a normal hour of the night. If ever witchcraft were to be abroad, if ever magic were to come into its own, it would be on such a night as this.

Slowly, her eyes still fixed upon the giant moon, the girl lifted her arms—slowly, slowly . . . reaching upwards and outwards towards the heavens like some primitive worshipper from the very dawn of history . . . .

'Bloody Christ almighty . . . !'

Piggy's shriek burst from her as her outspread fingers encountered Imogen's shrinking flesh . . . and in the ensuing confused medley of rage, and outrage, and useless apology, it was amazing that the whole household wasn't awakened.

They weren't, though. Perhaps noises at night seem louder to the perpetrators than they do to others. Anyway, no one came down . . . no one intervened to demand explanations, or to say calm down, take it easy, or to take one side or other in the furious battle.

Furious, but not, actually, a battle; for they were on the same side, right from the start. Imogen sympathised totally with Piggy's anger, and was fully conscious of the unforgivable injury she had unwittingly inflicted: consumed by guilt, she attempted to explain to excuse and to apologise all at once, in a confused, incomprehensible jumble: 'I never meant . . .' 'I wouldn't for worlds . . .' '. . . and from then on I felt I had to stay hidden . . . . Oh, Piggy, Piggy, *please* try to understand . . . .'

*

Piggy's face was pale as pudding in the moonlight, and Imogen tried to recall, like something in a dream, how beautiful it had been a few minutes ago. On the whitish forehead sweat gleamed, and from the contorted mouth came toads, in the form of insult after insult.

Imogen had always known that Piggy disliked her; but never before had she grasped the virulence of that dislike, nor the reason that lay behind it.

Partly, of course, it was that she, Imogen, was Ivor's wife, and during her year or more of unrequited love, Piggy had had plenty of time to observe, from her vantage-point on campus, all the ways in which her hero's wife was unworthy of him, and to collect evidence (albeit mostly hearsay) of the woman's inadequacies. Fair enough: any girlfriend worth her salt will do as much.

But it hadn't stopped there. After Ivor's death, the girl's natural grief and shock had been compounded by a new and unprecedented factor: she had heard, somehow, of the same rumour that Teri had heard: the two of them had got together on it, talked it over, come to a joint decision. Between them (she hissed, her lips grey and drawn in the moonlight)—between them, they would get Imogen hanged; yes, they would, capital punishment would be back just in time . . . .

'. . . but that's silly . . .' Imogen protested weakly, just as she had protested to Teri. 'I mean, I can *prove* that I wasn't . . .'

'Proof! . . . Proof . . . !' Piggy mouthed the word as if it was an obscenity. 'You'll find that it's too late for proof now, Mrs B. You've left it too long. By now, even your own family know that you did it! Yes, they do . . . !'

She faced Imogen with blazing eyes and fists white to the knuckles. Imogen, for some reason found herself giving a short, breathless little laugh.

'What, Herbert and all?' she asked. Really, it was too absurd. 'Well, why haven't they mentioned it, then? Why haven't they accused me . . . ?'

Piggy looked at her with narrowed, shining eyes.

'Because they're frightened, that's why. They're scared. They know you're mad, you see. They've known it for weeks now, and so they're frightened. They don't know what you might do next.'

21

Perhaps Cynthia wasn't quite the right confidante to have chosen. Sitting there, her pink bedjacket clutched around her with one white hand, while the other held a piece of toast, motionless, half-way to her parted lips, she looked as if these last revelations had been altogether too much for her. Imogen felt sorry, and a little ashamed. But then, who else was there, in all this household, to whom she could have turned? Robin, who would have laughed at the story, and saved it up to tease Piggy with next time he felt inclined? Or Dot, who would have said, But those curtains are supposed to overlap, how could there have been a crack? Or Herbert, who would have set himself to proving that it wasn't his fault, and that even if it had been . . .

It was at this point in her musings that Imogen realised that Cynthia, far from being overwhelmed, was absolutely loving it. Breakfast in bed and a scandal of these dimensions—even in the Rich Man's Paradise you don't get more than that.

'I knew it! I knew it!' She exclaimed—an assertion which Imogen took as a form of applause rather than a statement of fact—'I knew it! And, Imogen, like I said at the beginning, it explains everything. The handwriting, I mean . . . . You know how it is when you're in love . . .' her eyes took on a rapt, reminiscent look. 'There was a geography master we once had, I'll never forget him. He had a little brown moustache, and his eyes sort of crinkled when he told you off . . . . Oh, I thought he was gorgeous, though I daresay I wouldn't look at him now . . . . Anyway, for two whole terms I practised making my handwriting just like his—sort of flattened, with the "t's" just like the "r's", you know. I made a very good job of it actually, the other girls used to bribe me to write "Excellent" in red ink at the end of their homework, so that when the form-mistress looked through their exercise books for end-of-term reports, she'd . . . It was a sort of sacrilege, I sometimes felt, to let my love be used for such ends . . . but anyway, you see what I mean. That's how it must have been for poor Piggy . . . . Oh, I understand it all so well . . . !'

So did Imogen. There certainly was something in what Cynthia said. While writing forged deliberately for some extraneous purpose would indeed betray signs of artificiality and over-careful penmanship, it could well be that writing imitated out of love . . . out of the need to incorporate into one's very soul every gesture, every mannerism of the loved one . . . this might be a very different matter. The only puzzle was, how had Piggy ever come across any samples of Ivor's handwriting? It wasn't as if she was one of his own students.

Cynthia treated this objection with the scorn it deserved. For Heaven's sake, hadn't Imogen ever been in love? Of course Piggy would have laid hands, somehow, on things he had written with his own hand . . . . Probably locks of his hair, as well . . . .

'Yes, all right,' Imogen bowed to Cynthia's superior expertise with good grace— 'Yes, I suppose she would . . . lots of the students got crushes on him like that, it was always happening. Poor kid, I hope he threw her a kind word now and again . . . .'

'Well, but surely . . . ?' Cynthia was beginning; but then, apparently, thought better of it, for she went on, 'I tell you what, Imogen, would you like me to talk to her? I mean, it's obviously all nonsense, all this about you having murdered poor Ivor, but all the same, one can't help wondering what ever gave her such an idea? It may sound conceited, but I can't help feeling that if I asked her . . . I wouldn't be surprised if it turns out that she's really been in love with Teri all along, and that's why she's backing him up in his crazy story . . . .'

*

Actually, it was the other way round. When Cynthia returned, like an explorer with a bag of gold, from her successful interview with Piggy, the first thing that became clear was that it had been Piggy, not Teri, who had initiated the 'crazy story': and while she was in it for pure revenge, he (like any other middle-man) was in it for money and status. Money, of course, for its own sake, and status as a one-time boyfriend trying to get back into her favour.

No wonder he had proved so inept a blackmailer. All his 'information' and his 'proofs' were at second-hand, fed to him by Piggy. She'd have done better, really, to have done her own dirty work—apart from anything else, if she had done it, it wouldn't have been dirty. Revenge is one of the purest of all motives, untainted as it is by any thought of personal gain.

*

Cynthia seemed to have done her job well. Her boast of having 'this rapport thing' with the young was evidently not wholly unfounded—or maybe it was that her uninhibited and uncritical delight in anything the least bit shocking would have put almost any malefactor at his ease, young or not.

Anyway, whatever her techniques, they'd certainly worked. She'd managed to corner Piggy after lunch with a minimum of fuss and protest, and had succeeded in extracting from her some surprisingly detailed and intimate confessions.

'And I promised I wouldn't breathe a word to you about any of it,' Cynthia explained, 'so let's go up to your room and lock the door . . .' and the demands of loyalty thus satisfied, here the two of them now were, Cynthia reclining at ease on Imogen's bed as she talked, while Imogen sat leaning forward, all attention, in the basket-chair under the dormer window. While the afternoon light faded, and the draught from the window whistled silently against her neck, Imogen learned, with relief, everything that Cynthia had to tell.

Relief, because the story turned out to be a pathetic rather than a sinister one: a silly teenager, in the throes of calf-love, and half-crazed with shock and grief, thrashing around for something or someone to blame for the tragedy.

The 'someone' was not far to seek.

'She really did think you were at the hotel that night, you

know, Imogen,' Cynthia explained. 'She actually heard them saying so. You see, she was hanging about outside the hotel half the evening, hoping to get a glimpse of Ivor as he came in or out; and when she finally summoned up the courage to go inside and ask if he was still there, she heard all about it. The staff were all whispering and laughing about it— how you'd been chasing him all over the hotel. Obviously, it must have been some stupid mistake . . . but how could she have known that? Besides, by that time, she must have been pretty exhausted and wrought-up anyway . . . she'd started at crack of dawn, hitch-hiking up there in hopes of getting in to his lecture, but of course it was no good, it had all been booked-up for months, and anyway it wasn't for the general public at all. You can understand how she must have felt . . . .'

Imogen agreed that she could. So far, it all sounded silly, and sincere, and utterly plausible. Except, of course, this business about the hotel staff saying they'd seen her, Imogen. 'How could they have? I just simply wasn't there,' she insisted.

'Oh, I know you weren't, darling,' Cynthia hastily assured her. 'Of course I know—but I didn't want to argue with her. I mean, she might have turned huffy or something, and not told me the rest . . . .'

Which God forbid. So all right, then: there Piggy was, in the hotel foyer, her eyes out on stalks watching for Ivor every time the revolving doors revolved, and her ears filled with voices that she imagined were talking about Ivor's wife . . . .

Saying what about her?

Why, that earlier in the evening she had been in there

making a scene. Phoning up to Ivor's room, refusing to take 'No' for an answer, pushing her way past lift-man and porter and racing along the hushed, lush corridors to batter and plead at his locked door . . . quite a drama it had been, by all accounts, and Piggy no doubt had listened avidly.

Still, tangling with Ivor's wife (even in such propitious circumstances as these) was no part of Piggy's programme; and so, after hanging about uncertainly a little longer, she'd decided to put Plan B into operation: to be found, by chance, thumbing a lift at the side of the very motorway along which Professor Barnicott happened, by chance, to be driving home. The fact that it was a two-hour walk to the chosen rendezvous; that she had no idea whether her hero would be driving back tonight or tomorrow morning; and that it never stopped pouring with rain for one single second throughout the whole operation—none of this deterred her in the least . . . indeed, it only added to the glamour and excitement of the thing. Imogen pictured her standing there by the dark motorway as she had stood tonight beneath the moon, entranced, seeing and yet not seeing the cars that flashed past through the downpour, while her eyes, her whole soul, were all the time focused on another car, a non-car, a car that wasn't there: a car, though, that must come into sight sooner or later, for this was his way home. Standing there, she must have been unaware of the cold, of her soaked clothes. She would have been warmed through and through by her dreams: dreams of the magic car coming into sight . . . slowing down; of the magic face leaning out, first curious, then (who knew?) alight with recognition. Dreams, too, of what might follow . . . lurid, glorious, improbable dreams, alternating with terrible, searing nightmares . . . that he would be cool . . . preoccupied . . . bored with her company . . . ? Dreams, in fact, encompassing every conceivable possibility, good or bad, except the possibility that as she stepped forward, hand raised, he should suddenly and furiously accelerate, swerving at ninety miles an hour on to the wrong side of the road, covering in a few seconds the black quarter-mile, gleaming with rain, which separated her from the slow, shuddering crash which would echo in her head for the rest of her days.

*

Well, of course his wife had been the cause of it! Raving and carrying on like that at the hotel—what else could have upset so experienced and confident a driver as Professor Barnicott to that degree? Thus Piggy had reasoned; and then, later, when the news began to filter round the Campus that Professor Barnicott's wife had deliberately lied to the Press about the date of his accident . . . had pretended, for a whole day, that he was still alive . . . had denied having been at the hotel at all on that fateful night, although she had been positively seen there by half a dozen of the staff—why, the sinister implications of it stared you in the face. Obviously, the woman had somehow engineered the whole thing, either driving along with him and by some means escaping just in time, or else, maybe, administering some sort of drug before he set out . . . .

Something, anyway. It was obvious. Teri thought it was obvious, too.

Well, he would, wouldn't he? The aspiring boyfriend trying to win favour in the eyes of his love . . . . As Cynthia pointed out, it was all perfectly natural and understandable. Rather sweet, really, when you thought about it.

'Charming!' agreed Imogen, thinking about it. 'And so he helped her worm her way into my home on false pretences, so that she could collect further "evidence" against me? Spy on me, in fact?'

'That's right,' agreed Cynthia amiably, 'and actually, Imogen, that's one reason she was so upset to find that you were spying on her. I mean, it made it so confusing. She felt she just didn't know where she stood.'

'Well! Too bad . . . !' Imogen was beginning, and Cynthia took her up eagerly.

'Yes, she has had bad luck, hasn't she, poor girl? I'm so glad you see it that way, I was sure you would in the end. Because the thing is, Imogen, she's dreadfully, dreadfully unhappy. I mean, she did really love him—'

'I'm sure she did. So did I. But I'm not making that a reason for persecuting her. I do hope, Cynthia, that you tried to make her see things a bit more rationally? I mean for her own sake, too. All this lying and fantasy—it's an obsession she's got, and it can't be doing her any good. She must be made to snap out of it. After all, it's months now since he died.'

'Four months,' interposed Cynthia; and though her tone was neutral, her facts correct, Imogen knew exactly what she meant.

She didn't mean it unkindly, but she meant it: that Piggy, for all her faults and follies, was nevertheless mourning Ivor more adequately than Imogen herself was.

Grief is a strange malady. From what other illness would your friends—even the best of them—actively discourage you from recovering?

There was just one last point to clear up, and then—as Cynthia had said—everything would be explained. Where did Robin fit into the picture? For it was he, not Teri, who had introduced the girl into the house that Christmas eve.

For the first time since embarking on her narrative, Cynthia looked a little uneasy.

'Oh, well, you know what Robin is,' she said off-handedly, and Imogen did not press the matter further. Because, of course, it was true, she did know what Robin was. Who better?

22

'Mummy, where's Minos?'
'Daddy, have you seen Minos?'
'Granny, we can't find Minos, he isn't anywhere.'

Useless to explain to them (as Dot was conscientiously doing) what a big, sensible cat Minos was, and that he must have gone for a walk by himself.

'Cats don't go for walks!' the boys protested indignantly and in unison. 'Only dogs go for walks!'

'Do you think he's gone back to Twickenham? Do you think he hated it here?' enquired Vernon, with a mixture of curiosity and concern. 'Could a cat find his way, all along by the railway line . . . ?'

'Of course it could!' Timmie interjected knowledgeably. 'There was a cat I read about who . . .'

'Silly! That was just a story . . . !'

'It was not a story! It was in the paper. And when at last, all footsore and tired, it got to the gate that led into its own field, it—'

'It didn't.'
'It did.'
'Didn't.'

'Did.'

And there, to the relief of the adults concerned, the matter was allowed, temporarily, to rest.

*

How perverse children were. After all the fuss about wanting Minos here—all the tears and the pleadings: and after all the trouble Imogen had gone to, fetching him all the way from Twickenham, their reception of the creature when they encountered him in the kitchen the following morning had been lukewarm to say the least.

'Oh, Minos is here,' Vernon had commented, glancing for a moment from his plate of cornflakes: and, 'Granny, you won't let Minos get at my goldfish, will you?' Timmie had demanded.

'It's not your goldfish,' Vernon remarked, 'it's all-of-us's goldfish.'

'It is my goldfish! I thought of the name for him. I thought of calling him Goldie.'

'Goldie isn't a name, it's only a—'

*

And so on and so on. Imogen had felt quite absurdly disappointed. All the way home on the train, and lugging the cat-basket through the dark streets, she had buoyed herself up with thoughts of the children's surprise and delight when they woke up in the morning and found their pet actually here; she'd pictured the squeals of rapture, the hugs and kisses of joy and gratitude.

Nothing of the sort. After that one perfunctory exchange at breakfast, they had taken no further notice of the cat whatsoever. All day they had played their usual games, watched television, and squabbled; and all day Minos had dozed in the best chair by the dining-room fire, getting out of it only once, to stalk, aggrieved, over to the second-best chair. This was when Robin turned up to make an issue of his own claims to the most comfortable seat.

You couldn't say that Minos was being a nuisance, exactly, but it did seem like a waste of time ever to have fetched him.

'I suppose I'll have to remember to get in some Kat-o-Meal,' Dot had remarked grudgingly, 'it's gone up, too, 6p for a small tin . . . .'

The children had been no more enthusiastic.

'Why me?' Timmie had grumbled when asked to fetch the bag of Kitty-Litter from under the stairs, 'why not Vernon?'

*

And after all this, now look at them. Just because the wretched cat had been missing for an hour or two before bedtime, they were both going crazy about him all over again. 'We must have Minos!' 'We can't go to sleep without Minos.' 'Oh, Granny, will Minos starve if he's out all night?'

'Don't be silly'—Imogen was quite sharp with them—'and considering you haven't even looked at him all day long, or bothered about him the least bit . . .'

'Oh, but Granny . . . !'

'Oh, Granny, we have. I've bothered about him, anyway.'

'And so've I, Granny. Granny, what do you think's happened to him?'

Their concern seemed every bit as genuine as their indifference had been. Those were real tears glistening in Timmie's eyes; and Vernon's skinny little arms, protruding from the outgrown sleeves of his pyjama jacket, pushed and prodded with pathetic fervour at the blankets and eiderdown of his bunk in case Minos was somehow secreted among them.

No, of course he wouldn't suffocate. No, of course he'll find his way back. No, cats never get drowned, they keep away from the water. Now, that's enough, darlings, that'll do, you must go to sleep now. Yes, of course I'll listen for him. Yes, of course I'll leave the larder window open . . . yes, of course he'll be here in the morning when you wake up . . . of course . . . of course . . . of course . . . .

*

But he wasn't. For a few moments, standing at the back door in the icy January dawn, calling and chirruping vainly into the inert, frost-bound silence of a winter morning, Imogen was tempted to tell them all a big lie. Tell them that Minos had come back, and was right now asleep on her bed in the attic. Then, they would lose interest totally and at once, and all the fuss would stop. Certainly, not a soul would bother to go all the way up to her room to look.

Still, you can't do this sort of thing. Not really. You just can't. And so—just as had happened with supper last night—breakfast was left half-eaten, the scullery door was slammed open and

shut constantly into the freezing north wind, and the house echoed with argument and lamentations.

Minos! Minos! Where've you got to? No, of course he couldn't
have . . . I never said . . . Yes you did . . . Minos! Mi-i-nos!

By lunchtime, Imogen had had enough; and more to give
them something to do than with any real hope of success, she
suggested they should both come out with her that afternoon
and search the neighbourhood.

By the time they set out, she was herself beginning to feel
a little anxious about the old cat. She should have kept an eye
on him during these first two or three days; but he'd seemed to
be settling down so nicely, not bothered a bit by his unfamil-
iar surroundings. And of course there wasn't actually anything
remarkable about him electing to spend a night out—or even
several nights in succession; but all the same, he was sixteen
years old, and the neighbourhood was strange to him.

It was cold, too, and getting colder. As they hurried along
the nearly-deserted roads, shoulders hunched against the wind,
she fancied she could smell snow in the air. Already, Vernon's
cheeks were blotchy with cold.

'Minos! Mi-i-i-nos!' they piped now and then, randomly, into
the wintry vastness of the suburbs, scanning, with eyes water-
ing in the cold, the grey, frostbound gardens and the greyer
roads, straight and bare, stretching endlessly into the wind.

'Mi-nos! Mi-nos!' The children's voices, thin as reeds through
their numbed lips, made Imogen feel curiously depressed. It
was all so pointless, of course Minos wouldn't come, he wasn't
there. A mounting sense of oppression, of growing anxiety,
seemed to be closing in on her, quite out of proportion to the

mislaying of a cat. Something in the grey, snow-laden air was filling her with a terrible foreboding.

'Granny, I'm cold. Shall we go home now?'

'My hands are freezing, Granny. Don't you think Minos might have got home by now, if we went back and looked?'

The two pinched little faces gazed up at her trustingly, half-guilty and half-hopeful. She watched heroism and common-sense chasing one another experimentally across the untried, baby brows.

It didn't do always to give the victory to common-sense.

'Let's just go down to the Lanes; all those dustbins out in the street are just what he might like. And then, if you're not too tired, we'll walk past Garvey's Boat-house . . . there are rats there, people say. Minos would love rats.'

Rats! Real, live rats! The prospect revived their flagging spirits briefly, but all the same, the detour was a mistake, as Imogen realised almost at once. They were already too tired, too cold; and then, to crown all, when the dejected little trio finally reached the boat-house, it was locked. With numbed hands, and half-sobbing with frustration, first Vernon and then Timmie shook and rattled the heavy padlock.

'It's not fair . . .' sobbed Vernon—or was it Timmie?— 'I knew we'd . . .'

'Stop it! Shut up! Listen!' interrupted Timmie—or was it Vernon?—anyway, the other one, the one that had stopped crying; and standing there, in a wind that seemed to come slanting from all directions at once round the old building, they all heard it, or fancied they heard it: a creaking, whining sound, that could be a cat mewing. Or a loose board, groaning against its neighbour. Or an old, weathered row-boat creaking on its supports. Or almost anything, actually.

Too cold and disheartened to persevere with the quest, Timmie and Vernon nevertheless complained bitterly when Imogen urged them homewards. Whining, grizzling, and waxing self-righteously sentimental about the just-possibly animate sounds they had heard, they dragged along beside her; and only when she said, losing patience: 'All right, let's go back then', did the complaints abruptly cease.

*

It was quite a job getting them to bed that night.

'Minos! Oh, poor, poor Minos!' they wailed; and could only be pacified by an escalating series of hasty, cobbled-together promises about tomorrow, and about the superhuman efforts that would be put into mounting a renewed search. Gradually, the protests diminished, and ceased altogether when Dot gave them each a banana to eat in bed. Usually, only apples were allowed after tooth-brushing; but, as Dot said, after such an upsetting day it couldn't really do their teeth any harm.

*

Altogether, Dot was showing herself surprisingly sympathetic about the whole affair. For one who had been reiterating for years that Minos ought to be put away, her concern was really quite touching. All through supper, and in the sitting-room afterwards, she seemed as if she couldn't leave the subject alone.

When had the cat last been seen? Had he eaten his Kat-o-Meal before disappearing? And where, anyway, was the cat-basket in which Imogen had brought him from Twickenham? It had been under the dresser in the kitchen yesterday morning, Dot could swear it had. Someone must have moved it—

And so on and so on. Even after the subject had been talked to a standstill, she remained in a curious, fidgety mood, turning the television on and then off again, sighing, picking up her book and laying it down; and presently just sitting, silent, and curiously intent, as if listening for something.

'Hush!' she said once, quite sharply, when Cynthia, laying down her embroidery, began telling the story of her recently-capped molar; and when Cynthia retorted, huffily, that of course, if no one was interested—Dot merely said 'Hush!' again, even more peremptorily.

By half past nine, Imogen had had enough, and went off to the kitchen to make some tea. She was surprised, and by no means pleased, to find Cynthia clicketty-clacking along behind her, hell-bent on helping.

Or so she had presumed. When people follow you out to the kitchen like this it usually is because they want to drift around putting things idly in the wrong places while you exert yourself to entertain them, and afterwards thank them effusively. Imogen was already bracing herself for the familiar ordeal when it was borne in on her that she had jumped to her conclusion on insufficient evidence: Cynthia wasn't going to help at all.

'Look, Imogen,' she was saying, in the hushed, exultant tones of one who has dire news to impart, 'look, it came this afternoon! by post! I didn't like to give it you with all the others.'

She was holding out, as she spoke, a brown manila envelope, slightly battered from its long-ish sojourn in the pocket of her dress.

'What, for me——?' and Cynthia had the grace to look a little shamefaced.

'Yes, well, I thought it was so odd, you see,' she explained, 'I mean, why should she be writing to you at all . . . ? And posting it in London, too: I can't think when she can possibly have been in London, because . . .'

Imogen was turning the letter this way and that under the light. She had seen, the moment Cynthia took the envelope from her pocket, that the writing on it was Ivor's—Piggy's, that is to say.

She took a knife from the dresser drawer, and slowly, with monstrous, mounting terror, she slit the thing open.

'What is it, Imogen?' Cynthia kept saying. 'What's the matter?' Too vain, even at this exciting moment, to put her reading-glasses on, she peered anxiously and without avail over Imogen's shoulder. 'What is it? . . . Why are you looking like that? . . . Oh, please, Imogen, say something . . . !'

And at last Imogen did.

'Come along,' she said, her voice sounding hoarse and strange even to herself, 'come along, we should have checked on this before . . . . Oh, what fools we've been . . . !'

*

Piggy was not in her room, but it didn't matter—indeed, it was best that she shouldn't be. It was easier—much, much easier—to scrabble through her private notes and papers without her. And anyway, it hardly took a minute—she was, after all, a student, and quite a conscientious one, and so there were samples of her handwriting everywhere.

*

None of it in the least like Ivor's. Why should it be?

Cynthia's theory had been plausible, and delightfully romantic: but it just happened not to have been true.

And now, with the implications of the thing staring them in the face, the two women leaned over the brief missive, the one all agog with curiosity, the other filled with a mad, sick hope that the message might somehow have changed since she last looked at it.

But it hadn't.

'I've taken my cat back,' it ran, 'and tomorrow I'll come for my grandsons.'

No signature, nothing. And as Imogen stood there it slowly dawned on her that 'tomorrow', in a letter arriving by post, means 'today'.

23

'Gone? What do you mean, they're gone?' Dot was staring at Imogen blankly. 'But they can't be gone. I said good-night to them only . . .'

And then, at last, it sank in. The rushing, and the uproar, and the panic began.

'Hiding . . . ? But how . . . ?'

'Out? Oh, but they'd never . . .'

'Oh no . . . ! How could they . . . .'

*

Police? Apparently (so someone seemed to have been informed) in nine cases out of ten the police find the child perfectly safe somewhere in its own home.

The attics, then?

Of course I've looked in the attics.

The cellar?

Under the stairs?

Of course we've looked there. Looked there. Looked there. Looked there.

The cat. That wretched cat. They've been going on about it

all day. They wouldn't, surely . . . ?

No, of course they wouldn't.

Oh, aren't they naughty . . . !

'The police are on their way,' someone said, striding in from the hall; and at this Dot gave a little scream, and collapsed into a chair.

'Oh no. Oh no. I can't . . . I can't . . .' she kept sobbing, until someone seized her by the shoulders and yanked her to her feet.

'Shut up! Stop it!' ordered Herbert, giving his wife a peremptory little shake—and Imogen, watching, momentarily forgot her desperate anxiety in sheer amazement—'Now, come along, Dot, pull yourself together. We're going to Twickenham. Yes, now. The police will handle this end. What . . . ? Oh, don't be silly. I don't care a damn whether she's there or not, it's the kids that matter. Don't you realise, they're in danger? So shut up! And come on!'

And Dot, meek and dazed, and totally willing, followed her husband out of the room and out of the house, without even looking for her handbag.

Nonplussed though she was by this unprecedented performance on Herbert's part, Imogen couldn't help feeling that his notion of seeking the boys in Twickenham was a bit far-fetched, to say the least. It was true that they'd been squabbling, desultorily, about whether a cat could, or couldn't, find its way back to its old home over long distances: but a comfortable, theoretical squabble by your grandmother's fireside is one thing, a real-life journey, on a bitter winter night, by train, and bus, and tube, when you are only seven and eight years old, is surely another?

The dark, nearly deserted roads; the vast, cavernous main-line station . . . . Not to mention the money for the fares . . . .

No. They couldn't have.

Or could they? Did Herbert, perhaps, know his own sons best?

And if, at seven and eight years old, they would dare the night journey to Twickenham, then what else might they not dare?

*

The boat-house. The locked boat-house. With Minos in it, of course, sitting expectantly on the most comfortable bit of board, his yellow, censorious eyes fixed on the door whence rescue would come.

And with the rats in it, too, the exciting, delectable rats.

Not so delectable, though, on an icy winter's night, with no grown-up anywhere, and the deserted boat-house looming black and silent against the vast, unheeding sky.

It would be lonely, down there by the river, at this hour of the evening. Too cold for strollers, too late for stray commuters returning from work. The little boys would be quite, quite alone.

If they had gone out at all, they would surely have explored first the safer, more familiar areas, close to home?

*

It was just like the search for Minos all over again, only this time the suburban gardens were wells of impenetrable blackness, and the roads, white and hard in the moonlight, were completely deserted. The wind had dropped now, and the threat of snow no longer hovered in the air; but it was colder than ever—a harsh, biting cold, laced with dampness. Above the housetops hung the perfect disk of the moon, exactly at the full, but haloed, now, with a thin mist, and therefore casting no shadows. Everywhere was a level, changeless pallor, through which Imogen hurried as in a dream.

Hurried; but there was no point in hurrying, as she did not know where she was going. Every step she took could just as easily be taking her farther and farther from the children: but then again it might be taking her nearer. Walking was just as useless as standing still, but not particularly more so.

'Timmie! Vernon!' she called inanely, just as they had called 'Minos!' a few hours back. 'Timmee . . . Ver-non . . . !' She knew, of course, that they wouldn't answer because they weren't there, just as Minos hadn't been there, and so then she moved on, round the next corner, along the next road.

Twice—three times—helpful householders popped their heads round their front doors and asked could they do anything, but of course they couldn't. Have you seen two little boys, seven and eight years old? No, they were afraid not. Not two little boys. Not two little boys. No. Oh no. I'm sorry . . . .

Once, an old lady raised a brief, wild hope by explaining how she'd seen one little boy, carrying a basket of summun' . . . but the spurious moment of excitement was short-lived.

'Ah, don't be daft, Gran, that was Ron with the fish'n chips, dontcher remember? Besides, it was hours ago, tea-time . . .' and Imogen, thanking them, wandered on.

'Ver-non! Tim-mee!'

*

The boat-house, when she reached it, was exactly as she had pictured it—black, silent, and utterly deserted. Locked, too, of course, just as it had been this afternoon. The padlock was beaded now with half-frozen moisture, stinging to the touch. She shook it, senselessly, as a sort of ritual. Look, God, I'm doing something.

'Ver-non! Tim-mee!'

It took courage to shout in this deserted place, where your voice creaked like bats' wings among the empty wooden buildings, but she forced herself to do it.

'Ver-non! Tim-mee!'

*

'They went that-a-way, lady,' volunteered the sly-looking fifteen-year-old who ought to have been at home this winter night, not prowling around the deserted out-houses on the water-front. 'Yeh, thassit. Along that way—' he gestured vaguely towards the beginnings of the tow-path. 'They was running,' he added, with a certain relish, and stood watching Imogen with interest as she pounded away into the night. He'd never seen a woman run like that; as old as Ma she musta bin, or older.

A few hundred yards farther on she slowed her pace. How did she know, after all, if the boy was speaking the truth? He might have been making it all up for fun. Or maybe he was just being obliging, people love to say Yes rather than No when you ask them something, and anyone could tell that Imogen had wanted him to have seen the children.

Not to have seen them running, though. Running, perhaps in terror, alongside the black menacing water, deeper and wider than ever it seemed by day. What could they have seen, or imagined they had seen, that they should run thus blindly in a direction away from the town, away from human habitation, into the hollow, moonlit night?

'Tim-mee! Ver-non!'

Her voice was ridiculous under the vast sky, it reached nowhere, the syllables skimming feebly over the black water to be lost, sucked down, in the dark currents about half way over, never even reaching the opposite shore.

On she went, sometimes running, sometimes walking, into the bland, shadowless spaces of the night stretching palely as far as she could see.

'Tim-mee! Ver-non!'

The sounds drained away across the flat, dim water-meadows; tangled and lost themselves among the black clusters of reeds at the water's edge; and not so much as an echo of her own voice came back to her under the moon.

24

'Is it still following us?' asked Timmie tremulously. 'Is it, Vernie?'

It was years since Timmie had called his brother 'Vernie'—or, indeed, had turned to him for an opinion about anything whatever. Vernon, although terribly frightened, felt a little glow of pride.

'No—no, I don't think so,' he answered, looking back along the moonlit tow-path. 'I don't think it can be, Timmie,' he added, more confidently. 'I mean, if it was a ghost—and of course it can't be, there's no such things as ghosts—but if it was a ghost, then it would have caught us up by now, it could go much faster than we can.'

It was the wrong thing to say. The image it conjured up of the thing gaining on them with huge, effortless strides along the pale, glimmering tow-path, was too much for Timmie. He began to sob. 'Oh no . . . Oh no . . . .'

'But of course it isn't a ghost,' Vernon assured him, squeezing his hand—it must have been years, too, since the little boys had condescended to walk hand-in-hand—'there's no such things as ghosts, Timmie, really there isn't. And it didn't look like a ghost, did it?'

*

Not to start with, it didn't. It hadn't talked like a ghost, either, at the beginning. It had talked quite sensibly. In fact, the whole thing had started so easily, so innocuously: it had never occurred to the little boys as they tiptoed, guilty and excited, out of the front door, that they were embarking on an adventure on this sort of scale. They'd known, of course, that they were being naughty, that they were supposed to be in bed: but then they'd been promised that it would only take a minute or two; and that it was urgent, because Minos might run away if they didn't hurry; he was only just up the road, but no one could catch him, he wouldn't come to people he didn't know . . . .

It wasn't as if it was a stranger who'd persuaded them. If it had been, then naturally they wouldn't have gone. They both knew very well that one doesn't go off with strangers in any circumstances, no matter how good the pretext.

But surely someone who has been to the house, who has stood on the steps talking to Mummy and Daddy, who has brought bars of chocolate, isn't a stranger? And so when Minos turned out not to be just up the road after all, they felt no great qualms about going a little farther, as far as the Gardens. Lots of cats gathered there (so their informant assured them) alongside the railings, at just this time in the evening, because old ladies came to feed them. Minos, no doubt, would be among the rest.

But he wasn't; and so one thing led to another, and presently they were down by the boat-house—uneasy by now, but too shy to protest. If Imogen had arrived there just one hour earlier, she would have seen them.

'It was the picnic that made me start to run,' confided Timmie to his brother as they plodded hand in hand through the moonlight. 'All that about the picnic . . . . No real person goes for a picnic in the middle of the night.'

'No.' Vernon weighed the point up anxiously. 'Still, Timmie, it doesn't prove it was a ghost. I mean, I don't suppose even ghosts . . .'

'And all that about Grandpa expecting us,' continued Timmie apprehensively. 'I didn't like it. I mean, Grandpa's dead, he can't be expecting us . . . .'

'Of course he can't . . . it was just . . . silly,' affirmed Vernon, as confidently as he was able. He was still feeling very frightened. Because, if it wasn't a ghost, then why did it go on like that about Grandpa waiting for them in the meadows by the river? 'No real person would go for a picnic in the middle of the night,' Timmie had said, and of course he was right. No real person would. A river-picnic, too . . . would Grandpa, too, be a ghost when he came to join them, rowing silently, moth-white, across the dark water, the ghost-oars making no sound as they dipped and rose . . . ?

*

'I think perhaps we'd better run some more,' he said to Timmie, in a tight little voice, 'just to keep ourselves warm'—and hand-in-hand they jogged onwards once more, towards nothing and nowhere, under the light of the moon. By the time Imogen passed the same spot, nearly an hour later, there was no tiniest trace of the small footsteps on the rutted, frozen path; no faintest echo of the timid, childish voices lingered any longer on the still night air.

*

Imogen had long since given up calling the children. It seemed terribly dangerous, somehow, to be thus broadcasting their names at random into the infinite spaces of the night. Now and again she glanced furtively at the black, faintly stirring water out there beyond the reeds, imagining, sometimes, that among the small silvery ripples she could detect a brighter swirl of disturbance, a turmoil of ghastly happening. But of course it was never anything; a small fish rising, perhaps; or a floating twig, revolving slowly into silver light. And other times, peering off towards the left instead of to the right, her eyes would scour the grey water-meadows for two black dots trudging away into the white moonscape; and always she saw them, not two merely, but dozens of them, hundreds, dancing, merging, vanishing in front of her eyes. They were there, they weren't there, bobbing about and re-appearing, drowning in the moonlight as in an infinite sea . . . .

*

Suddenly, there was a woman walking briskly towards her along the tow-path. An elderly—yes, an old woman—wearing a head-scarf . . . . Imogen stopped dead, for a moment, in utter amazement. Then, clearing her throat, she hurried forward.

'Excuse me,' the woman said, coming to a halt as Imogen drew near. 'Have you seen two little boys, seven and eight years old? I seem to have lost them.'

25

Afterwards, Imogen could have kicked herself for not realising at once who the woman must be. What an extraordinary coincidence! was all she could think at the time; and even when the stra-nger, in the very next sentence, referred to the lost children as 'my grandsons', Imogen still only thought, dazedly, that the coincidence had become more amazing still.

It was the cowslips that got her mind functioning again.

'I wanted to show them the cowslips,' the woman said, sadly. 'Of course, I know really it's the wrong time of year, and naturally daytime would be better. But it's only a little way on from here, and it's a very special place . . . it's where their grandfather and I used to come in summer time, when we were young, and the cowslips were out, and the cuckoos calling. Oh, forty years ago it must be now, since he and I were there together! I wanted it to be me, and no one else, who showed it to our grandsons.'

'Our grandsons.' Hers and Ivor's. Her own true grandsons, by blood and birth. Not Imogen's at all.

What a fool I've been, thought Imogen. Why did I never guess that after his death, Ivor's first wife might be turning up again? Just as Cynthia, his second wife, had done. His first wife—Lena, yes, that was her name—why have I never given her a thought all these years? I knew—of course I knew—that she was still alive, somewhere—in a Home, wasn't it. Some kind of a Home . . . ?

Here Imogen stole an uneasy glance at her companion. They were walking side by side now, in the direction from which the woman—Lena—had been coming. She was taller than Imogen, and though she must be quite old (fifteen years older than Ivor, that made her seventy-four or five, Imogen quickly calculated) she walked briskly, and held herself very erect. Beneath the head-scarf wisps of grey hair escaped here and there; the fine, sculptured profile was pale in the moonlight, and the eyes—huge, luminous, deep-set eyes—were very bright. Once, she must have been very beautiful.

But this was no time for such speculations.

'Where . . . ? When did you last see them . . . ?' Imogen asked breathlessly, hurrying to keep up. 'The boys . . . ? How do you know this is the way they went . . . ?'

Lena smiled, a strange, contented smile: and Imogen was conscious of a small, inexplicable flutter of fear. How calm the woman was in the face of this crisis!—Too calm. And how smooth, how unlined, was the seventy-four-year-old face, washed by the moonlight! Almost like the face of a young girl.

Almost, but not quite. Imogen recognised in the bland, tranquil features that curious, unused quality, masquerading as youthfulness, of those who have spent long years in institutions.

'Don't worry,' Lena was saying, still smiling straight ahead into the moon, 'it's not far now—you'll see . . .' Unexpectedly, she gave a little laugh, and quickened her already brisk pace: 'Naughty little things—I told them to stay close to me, but you know what youngsters are! But I'm not worrying—they'll turn up soon enough at the picnic-place. That's always been a firm rule of mine with the children: 'If you get lost, go straight back to the picnic-place, and wait . . . !'

'Picnic-place . . . !' Imogen was beginning—and then decided to close her mouth, once and for all. Question and argument would only cause delay. In all this wide white landscape under the bowl of the sky, the only clue as to the children's whereabouts lay beneath that head-scarf, behind those shining eyes. All she could do was follow. In the journeys of the mad, sanity can only be a stumbling-block and a hindrance.

Quietly, the two trudged on. Quietly, Imogen took the side nearest the river, whence she could watch the black water, keep an eye on its faint, inscrutable eddies of pale light. So near was she, sometimes, that her coat brushed against the reeds with a dry, whispering sound.

It was clear that the first Mrs Barnicott had not, as yet, recognised the third one; and indeed, why should she? She had already become a more or less permanent hospital inmate long before Imogen had appeared on the scene, and neither had ever met the other. Imogen could see no point in revealing herself now; and indeed, the notion became steadily less and less inviting as they proceeded on their way and Lena began, in a bitter, clenched monotone, to confide her troubles—the prime cause of which, apparently, was her children's current stepmother, a woman called Imogen. A poisonous woman, a destroyer of family ties; a woman who had alienated her step-children, Dot and Robin, from their own real mother; and not content with this, was now intent on doing the same with the grandchildren.

"Granny," she's taught them to call her! "Granny"—and she no relation to them at all. Whereas I, who really am their grandmother—they hardly know me. I've only been allowed to see them a couple of times in all the months since I came out of hospital; and even then they weren't told I was their grandmother. It's wicked—it's cruel: and all the time it's my house they've been living in—the house Ivor and I bought when we married and went to live in Twickenham. I'm not even allowed there as a visitor any more—can you believe it? "I'm scared", my daughter says: "I'm scared to let the children be in the same house with you, Mother . . . ." What do you think of that? My own daughter, scared to leave her children with their own grandmother . . . ! She's not scared to leave them with the Imogen woman, though. Oh no, with her, it's "Granny" this, and "Granny" that . . . And calling out for her in the night . . . how do you think I felt when I heard a little voice calling 'Granny! Granny!' in the middle of the night, and it didn't mean me, it meant her. And she a total stranger, no relation at all . . . And when I, his real Granny, ran to the little boy, leaned over to kiss him, you know what he did?—he hit me, and screamed! Screamed and screamed, until she came to console him. If I could lay my hands on that woman . . . if I could get her by herself . . . just for one minute . . . even at my age . . . .'

*

Imogen was keeping very, very quiet: just saying 'Mm?' now and again, and 'What a shame', as they walked side by side in the moonlight. By this means, she tried not to exist, and yet keep the woman talking. Somewhere, buried deep among these miscellaneous grievances would be the map they were going to need tonight; the eerie, terrible moonlit map, with the children's whereabouts marked on it with an X.

*

'. . . and Dot—my own daughter Dot—is putty in her hands,' the bitter, powerful voice drove on. 'Between them, they saw to it that I wasn't invited even on Christmas Day. I'd bought presents for the children—I'd even looked out the old Father Christmas outfit that Dot herself used to be so thrilled by when she was a tiny girl, and her father came in all dressed-up, sprinkled with snow, and loaded with presents . . . . Those were the days when we were so happy still, Ivor and I . . . so happy . . . .'

There was a far-away look in the wild, brilliant eyes; and Imogen, cautiously, tried to bring her back to the matter in hand.

'And so what happened?' she prompted, 'About the Father Christmas outfit, I mean . . . ? Did someone wear it in the end?'

'Oh yes. Someone wore it, all right.' Lena gave a harsh laugh. 'I wore it! I had to sneak into the house secretly, though, to do so. I came in like a burglar that first time, through a window; but afterwards I used to come in whenever I liked, through the front door. Searching around the study, you see, I found my husband's keys, the bunch of keys he always used to carry; and luckily, the Twickenham key was among them as well. And so after that, you see, I was able to get into both the houses whenever I chose, without any of them knowing a thing about it. I was able to stay in the Twickenham house . . . look after my cat . . . .'

'But Christmas—the Father Christmas outfit?' Imogen once more ventured, and again Lena laughed, bitterly.

'Ah, yes. Christmas! My first Christmas out of hospital, and there they all were, eating the Christmas dinner that I hadn't been invited to; enjoying themselves without me. I'll give them a surprise, I thought, I'll give them the shock of their lives, and please the children at the same time. I had it all worked out: I'd change into the Father Christmas outfit in the study, while they were all still in the dining-room, and then, as soon as they'd finished their dinner, I'd make my entrance, just as Ivor used to . . . . All in my red cloak and beard, and with my arms full of presents . . . after that, they could hardly shut me out of the festivities, could they?

'But it didn't happen like that. I'll tell you.

'I was ready much too early—that was the thing. They were still in the dining-room eating, and so, to pass the time, I began looking through my old books, my Greek texts that I'd let Ivor have when he was young and poor. It was strange to be handling them all again . . . my precious leather-bound Sophocles . . . my complete works of Plato . . . and my own old Liddell and Scott, that I'd used ever since I was a student . . . . Of course, the print is too small for me now, my sight isn't what it was, but luckily I found in the desk a pair of reading-glasses that must have been Ivor's; but anyway, they seemed to suit well enough, and soon I was deep in the Bacchae.

'I don't know how much later it was—it seemed like only a few minutes—when suddenly, without warning, one of the little boys burst in—the littlest one. It was very sudden, I was engrossed in that lovely chorus that begins, "the white-footed dancers in the dewy midnight air" . . . at first, I could scarcely collect my wits. Still, I was delighted, of course, and I jumped up to hug him, to wish him a Happy Christmas from his very own real Granny—and do you know what happened? Do you know what he did? He ran away! Ran away, as if I was some kind of monster! That's what she's taught them—that I'm some kind of a monster! Where love should be, she has planted hate; instead of trust, she has inculcated fear. It was in that moment, as the child—my own grandson—rushed out of the room in terror, that I began to realise that if ever my grandsons were to learn to love me, I must get them right away from these people, if only for a few hours. I began to plan and scheme . . . how I could take them out for some sort of a treat or outing all by themselves, just me and them. That's how I meant it to be tonight . . . this picnic by the river . . . .'

Imogen caught her breath. Here—any moment now—would come the revelation she had been waiting for: where the boys were, and what they were doing. She waited, not daring to distract the speaker by so much as a murmur of enquiry.

But it is possible to be too tactful. Without the stimulus of question and comment from an involved listener, Lena began to lose the thread of what she was saying. Half a lifetime of stored-up bitterness is not conducive to clear, consecutive narration, and soon the multifarious grievances and injuries began to boil and seethe in unselective confusion, now one and now another bubbling randomly to the surface.

'. . . and you know something else? She's hidden my manuscripts. Buried them away in the attic, under mountains of
other stuff. They should have been in the bedroom, we always
kept our manuscripts in the bedroom, for safety. And so back
to the bedroom I brought them, back where they belonged.
Quite a job it was too, up and down those attic stairs with
armful after armful of papers—I was terrified that someone
would see me, though of course I was being as quiet and careful as I could.

'Half way through, I had a brain-wave. There was a black
cloak kind of thing hanging behind one of the attic doors, I
put it on and pulled the hood right up over my head so that
even if anyone did get a glimpse of me, I could still get away
without being recognised. I found out later that it belongs to a
girl who never speaks, so even if they'd actually challenged me,
it wouldn't have mattered: they all know that she's quite rude
enough not to answer when spoken to, I could have pushed past
them without a word, and no one would have been surprised
in the least.

'But in fact, no one did see me, at least I don't think so. I
got most of it done during one Sunday lunchtime, when they
were all downstairs. I loaded all the papers on to the big four-
poster bed, and then I drew the curtains round me like a little
fortress, and sorted it all out. It was amazing what I found:
notes, and articles, and translations that I'd forgotten all about.
And among all the rest—would you believe it?—I found my
book! My book on the Minoan scripts. The book that would
have made my name, I know it would, if only I'd been able to
finish it . . . . But after I married Ivor, I never again finished

anything . . . never. Sometimes, when I think of the career I might have had . . . the fame that was waiting, only just round the corner . . . .'

*

The catalogue of disappointment, spanning more than a quarter of a century, seemed as if it might go on for ever as they plodded forwards under the moon; but presently something in the quality of her companion's silence must have caught the speaker's attention, for she came to an abrupt standstill, and turned to peer full into Imogen's face. Floodlit under the moon, every feature must have been clearly etched.

Had this angry, embittered woman actually ever seen Imogen's face, during her secret peregrinations up and down the house? And, having seen it, would she still recognise it in this eerie half-light?

Imogen stared stonily ahead of her, and waited.

'I'm sorry, I'm boring you,' Lena apologised at last. 'It's so long, you see, since I've had anyone to talk to . . . you're very kind . . . . And do you mind, now, being rather quiet? We're almost there . . . .'

It was quite hard to keep up with the agile old woman as she swerved, suddenly, off the path, and struck away from the river into the moon-drenched meadows. The tufts of withered grass were black and treacherous in the moonlight, but it was Imogen, not the older woman, who stumbled as they made their way, swift as a dream, towards the black, frost-bitten hedgerow where, in summer, the dog-roses would be blooming, and the cow-parsley, nearly three feet tall, would be scenting the warm air.

On the icy grass, by the light of the mist-ringed moon, Ivor's first wife sat down . . . lay back with a sigh of contentment and closed her eyes.

'It's funny,' she said, 'I can never imagine it not being summer in this place. Always, the sun is shining, hot and golden . . . always, I can hear the insects humming in the long grass . . . always, the cowslips are in bloom. Here, right here, is where we always used to come, Ivor and I . . . here, in the long grass, we lay like gods together, and the scent of the may-trees was everywhere . . . .

'Oh, he was an Adonis in those days . . . a golden boy! He came to my lectures, you know, my lectures on Minoan Crete, that's when I first noticed him; in the front row of the lecture-room, and his auburn hair like the sun. I was amused, at first, at the way he never took his eyes off me; and later, when he began coming to me for tutorials, I noticed that his writing was growing more and more like mine as the weeks went by, until at last you couldn't tell which was which.

'Even then, I was still only amused—and a little flattered, too, of course—well, what woman wouldn't be? To have your very handwriting immortalised by love . . . .

'But he was shy in those days—so shy. I never dreamed it would come to anything—how could it, with him a first-year student not yet twenty, and I a thirty-four-year-old lecturer, just coming up to the peak of my career? . . . Perhaps I should never have let it come to anything . . . so many years' difference in our age . . . but I loved him, you see. Loved him wildly, passionately, just as he loved me. Besides, I was afraid of what he might do—so young and wild! He used to say that if ever I left him, he would throw himself off Cobley Tower . . . .'

And would too, Imogen reflected drily, if enough people had been gathered below to watch . . . but aloud she said nothing, and the older woman continued:

'. . . A love like ours . . . how can it be wrong? How can it, no matter what a person's age may be? . . . Listen, isn't that a cuckoo? Do you know, just for a moment, I thought I heard a cuckoo. How silly I am! How could there be a cuckoo, at night, and in the winter . . . ?'

She laughed, a small, uneasy laugh, and half sat up, raising herself on her elbow. Her head-scarf had become dislodged, and the tumble of grey hair, blanched by the moonlight, could just as easily have been bright gold; golden hair falling about her, just as it must have fallen all those years ago when Ivor, laughing, had pulled out the pins and combs that held the severe, shining bun in place, and changed his love, all in a moment, from a brilliant Classics lecturer to the girl of his dreams.

Imogen tried once more to bring her back to the present.

'The boys?' she urged anxiously, 'The little boys . . . your grandsons? We can't just sit here . . . .'

'Oh dear! Yes!' Lena sat up hurriedly, and passed her hand across her forehead. 'Yes, they should be here by now . . .' She peered round her into the blurred, empty radiance that stretched as far as the eye could see.

'Oh dear, they are being naughty! I told them that this was where we'd be having the picnic. Perhaps, if I get out the food . . . ?'

*

It looked like rubbish more than food; but it was food. A doughnut, complete with crumpled paper bag; a couple of tired cheese sandwiches; and a digestive biscuit, wrapped in newspaper. Lena laid them, wrappings and all, on the moonlit grass. A battered packet of peanuts came next; an orange, and a flattened piece of chocolate: she gazed at the meagre, messy little display uneasily.

'I'm sure there was more than this . . . ?' she muttered, rootling again in the depths of her winter coat. This time, she brought out some liquorice, a bath-bun, and a greasy little packet of crisps, already half-finished. Laid out under the moon, the collection looked like the contents of an over-turned dust-bin.

The old woman looked at it, puzzled, as if not quite sure what was wrong.

'We used to have hot rolls, of course,' she said, sadly. 'Lovely fresh, crisp rolls . . . but of course the shop is gone now, there's a launderette where the baker used to be. And I used to bring chicken wings sometimes, and ham, and Ivor would come leaping towards us through the grass like Dionysus, with a bottle of wine in either hand . . . Oh, he loved me, then! He loved me . . . .'

In the moonlight, her eyes glittered with a kind of joy: 'Yes, he loved me! That's something I've got that she will never have, because, after he stopped loving me, he never loved anyone . . . .'

Was is true? Imogen looked at the grey old woman, wraith-like under the moon, and tried to picture her in her golden prime, forty years ago. To picture Ivor loving her, deeply, passionately, through all the years when he was capable of loving; and then moving on, into a brighter, colder, more exciting world . . . .

*

Imogen clutched her coat about her. Her teeth were chattering.

'The boys . . . ?' she protested, yet again. 'The children . . . ? Surely they'll never find us here . . . ? They never could have thought you really meant . . .' suddenly, with terrible premonition, she turned on her companion:

'What did you tell them? Please, please try to remember! What did you really tell them . . . ?'

*

At first, under the pale, eldritch light, she thought the older woman's face was contorted with fury. It looked grotesque, deformed, rutted with evil. Then, all at once, she realised that Lena was merely on the verge of crying. The old, tired mouth was working with emotion, her whole face twitched with the effort of control. This, then, was the face that Vernon must have seen leaning over him that night: his real, own grandmother trying to fight back the tears of love and longing . . . .

This time, the fight was successful; with a huge effort, the old woman recovered herself, blinking back the moonlit tears before they could fall. She even smiled a little, uneasily.

'Tell them . . . ? What did I tell them . . . ? Why, as I've been saying, I told them . . .'

Her voice wavered, stumbled into silence; and now, for the first time, Imogen saw a look of fear flicker in the great luminous eyes.

'I . . . I . . .' Lena stared to left and right, then left again, as if scanning a page of print: as if the answer lay scrawled in vast black letters across and across the moonlit wastes.

'I told them . . . well, naturally, I told them . . .'

And now Imogen saw the old lips quivering, watched the terror darkening in the brilliant eyes.

'I told them—Oh, what a fool I am! Oh, how could I have done such a thing! I said just now, didn't I, that I couldn't imagine it not being summer in this place?—well, I told them—I think I told them—that they could bathe! Over there, in the river—I told them they could swim until I called them . . . . I forgot, you see, that it was winter, and night-time . . . . I just didn't remember . . . . Oh, they'll be cold. So cold!'

It was Imogen who was on her feet first; gasping, stumbling, almost sobbing in her terror as she raced desperately in the direction of the river: raced with all her strength, her heart thundering, her breath almost gone; but even so the older woman overtook her easily, skimming over the ragged winter fields like an athlete, like a goddess, like something immortal under the immortal moon. And as the flying figure reached the water's edge, there came a wild, unearthly cry of panic and despair:

'Come out, darlings, come out! You'll die of cold . . . ! Dot . . . Robin . . . come out . . . !'

Imogen was too far behind to hear that the names echoing through the freezing night were the names of children long grown-up; and by the time she had caught up, whatever Lena had seen in the black water could be seen no more; there was only the dark, quiet river, gleaming eerily under the moon. And right here, at the water's edge, face-down among the shallows, lay Lena, just as she had fallen.

*

It wasn't drowning, the doctors said afterwards; Imogen had pulled her out in plenty of time. It was shock, over-exertion, and chill.

Though how she could have got a chill in all that golden summer sunshine, with the cowslips out, and with the cuckoos calling, the doctors were never able to explain.

They were never asked, of course: it would have been a crazy, idiotic question.

26

Vernon and Timmie weren't allowed to go to their grand-mother's funeral. As Dot pointed out, it wasn't as if they'd ever realised that Lena was their grandmother. And in any case (she insisted) they were still suffering from shock. Should be, anyway.

Actually, the little boys seemed to have recovered with remarkable speed from their frightening experiences of that night; they hadn't even caught cold. The police had picked them up on the tow-path less than a mile outside the town; and by the time Imogen reached the same spot, an hour or so later, they were already (had she but known it) safe at home, revelling in hot cocoa, hot-water-bottles, and such a degree of solicitous attention as they might never enjoy again. By the day of the funeral they were suffering less from shock than from a slight sense of anticlimax. People had stopped praising and hugging them for just being alive; and by now the story of their adventures (even as elaborated by Timmie) was beginning to bore even themselves. The funeral, with a real grave, and real earth being shovelled on to the coffin, would have provided a welcome distraction.

But Dot was adamant.

'They hardly knew her, they can't possibly feel any grief,' she asserted, cupping her hands round a mug of the hot coffee that Imogen had brewed to sustain them through the coming chilly ordeal by the grave-side in the icy wind. 'Even I, her own daughter, can't pretend to be sorry . . . it would be hypocrisy . . .' and with these words, Dot set her mug down with a jolt on the kitchen table, and burst into tears.

She had been crying like this, on and off, for three days now, and she herself would have been the first to admit that it was guilt, not grief, that was the cause.

'If only I'd visited her more often in hospital . . . If only I'd taken her side more . . . . If only I'd realised that after Dad left her she just couldn't help going to pieces . . . If only I'd sympathised when she had that first breakdown . . . when she started drinking . . . . If only . . . if only . . . if only . . .'

If only she'd been infinitely patient, infinitely understanding. If only she'd been a better daughter, a more saintly child . . . .

'Even at seven, I knew that something was wrong. I knew that Mother needed me, needed my support. I could see, even at that age, how unkind Dad was being to her . . . how unfair. I listened to their quarrels, I witnessed their fights and rows, and I could see very well that, every time, she was in the right, and he was in the wrong. She was good . . . so good . . . and he was bad and wicked; and yet he was the one that everybody loved—always! I used to lie in bed at night crying about the unfairness of it all—and all the time, the most terrible thing of all was that I knew, deep down in my heart, that I, too, loved him best; far, far better than I'd ever loved her. He was selfish, conceited, even cruel—and yet he was the one I loved. Always. And so did Robin. Robin adored him. As a little boy, Dad was his hero, he couldn't do enough to please him . . . to try to be like him . . . . And now he is like him'—here Dot's voice rose to a sort of howl—'and it's all my fault! I was his big sister . . . . I could have stopped it . . . .'

Such all-embracing guilt cannot be tackled head-on; the victim has to work through it at her own speed. For the third time in the past forty-eight hours, Imogen pointed out to her step-daughter that a little girl of eleven can hardly be held responsible for her four-year-old brother's psychological development; but Dot just shook her head despairingly.

'I could have saved him, I could,' she wailed. 'I could have guided him . . . helped him . . . and I didn't! Robin is all my fault . . .'

'Boasting again?—How it runs in the family.'

Robin's voice from the doorway made Dot jerk her head up, blinking at her brother with swollen, tear-filled eyes. 'I'm sorry to disillusion you, Sister-mine,' he went on, coming farther into the room and leaning his elbows on the back of a chair the better to harangue them. 'I'm sorry, but I'm not your fault at all. Or hardly at all. I'm her fault'—here he pointed a sudden accusing finger at Imogen. 'It's her! She dunnit! Always spoiling me . . . interceding for me with Dad . . . . Just like she was always spoiling him and interceding for him with the rest of the world. You did, Step, and don't deny it. You found yourself with a couple of psychopaths on your hands, and it was just your cup of tea, wasn't it? You encouraged all our most objectionable qualities and made us worse and worse, it was marvellous'—here he reached across and patted her on the shoulder approvingly. 'You're just a psychopaths' moll, that's what you are, Step. You'll be getting to work on Timmie next, just mark my words. He's another one. You can see it already—'

'He's not! Stop it! You mustn't say such horrible things . . . !'

Robin looked pleased at having succeeded in getting a rise out of his sister. He smiled.

'They're not horrible things at all. They're flattering. I only wish I could say as much for poor Vernon, but I'm afraid he takes after you, Dot. No one would ever guess that he comes of a long and distinguished line of successful psychopaths. A pity, poor lad; he'll never know what he's missing. He'll never know the glory, the triumph, of being always, in every situation, the one who doesn't care. The one who doesn't care can always make rings round the one who does, you know, because he has nothing to lose. It's like a fairy gift, lifting you high above the heads of other mortals. You look down at them pityingly . . . you watch them struggling away down there, tied hand and foot by the things they care about . . . and you feel as if you're flying . . . you feel like a god among men. That's why everybody loves us so much, why they let us get away with such a lot . . . it's because they recognise us as the nearest thing to a god that they will ever know . . . .'

'Don't-Care was made to care'—this was the best that Dot could manage in response to her brother's lyrical outburst. 'One has to care, Robin, or . . .'

Robin swung round on his sister.

'Look at you! You care—you care about every damn thing, and look where it's got you! And incidentally, look where it's got the people on the receiving-end of your caring, too. All those months of guilt and soul-searching about whether you ought to invite Mother to live with you—and what happens? You don't invite her. Just like I don't invite her. From Mother's point of view, there must have been damn-all to choose between your contortions of guilt and concern, and my straight-forward heartlessness. It all added up to not bloody having her. Didn't it?

'Not that it was your fault, actually, Dot. Nor mine. It was Dad's fault.'

*

Robin was right. Now that the whole sorry story had been pieced together, no one could have any doubt that it was Ivor himself—or rather, the glorified self-image that had served him for a self so long and so faithfully—who must be blamed.

*

He must have panicked, of course. After years of comfortably assuming that his first wife was going to remain safely tucked away in hospital for the rest of her days, the news of her impending discharge must have come upon him like a thunder-clap. Confronted with the appalling verdict that she was recovering . . . that the new drugs, the new treatments, and the new, more liberal regime within the hospital, had, in her case, worked, and rendered her capable of living outside, provided she had a supportive family to go to—he must have been knocked sideways.

A more honest man would have told them No, she hadn't a supportive family: a kinder one would have made some sort of effort to provide her with one. But Ivor could not bring himself to do either. He had immediately liked the image of himself as the head of a 'supportive family'—Imogen could imagine the way he would have charmed and reassured the superintendent, giving the impression of being the kindest, warmest, most concerned fellow in the world, with the kindest, warmest, most supportive family at his back.

A delightful picture of family devotion and solidarity: the only item left out being the fact that Ivor himself had not the slightest intention of ever being bothered with any of it ever again once he was safely through those swing-doors. He hadn't even bothered, it seemed (unless this was a piece of genuine forgetfulness) to warn his children that their mother would shortly be reappearing in their lives.

And so it was that Lena's first experience of the outside world was one of horrified rejection; first by her daughter, in a turmoil of guilt and indecision, and next by her son, who of course made short work of the problem, and without any guilt or indecision at all. He simply bundled his mother into his car and scorched northwards with her up the motorway towards the city where his father (so he had ascertained) happened to be giving some kind of a learned lecture that very week-end. Let him cope with her, the old scoundrel: it's his fault—in some such state of mind had he dumped his mother on the steps of the lecture-hall and fled, without even ascertaining that she would be allowed in without pre-arrangement.

She wasn't: a bitter disappointment, no doubt, if by this time she had been indulging delectable visions of revealing herself to her astounded ex-husband by rising to her feet with some brilliant question or comment from the body of the hall . . . .

*

'Mrs Barnicott' . . . 'behaving oddly' . . . at the hotel that evening . . . No wonder, poor woman, with her ex-husband, whom she still loved, dodging her from room to room . . . from lift to reception-desk and back again . . . doubling-back like a cornered fox as she hunted him up and down the long, lush corridors—probably, by now, with her grey hair coming adrift from its pins and combs and flying loose as if she was an aged Artemis, the Huntress Queen . . .

'Odd' could have been an understatement.

And in the end, after all this, Ivor had escaped her, scrapping his hotel booking without a word to anyone and blazing off along the motorway into the night.

*

Understandably, Piggy was reluctant to accept this revised version of events. She had naturally assumed, at the time, that the 'Mrs Barnicott' referred to by the hotel staff was the current one, and she wanted it to stay that way.

'Well, all right,' she allowed at last, grudgingly, 'but all the same, I'm bloody sure that someone was to blame. He was a super driver, he'd never have gone into a skid like that unless someone, somehow, had given him some sudden, terrible shock . . .'

*

Someone had, of course. Imogen could only hope, for the girl's own sake, that she would never find out who it was.

A frantic, love-crazed teenager, soaked with rain, wildly gesticulating from the dark verge of the motorway, her pale, bedraggled hair falling like seaweed across her obsessed, shining face . . . such an apparition could be a little confusing to a man who is at the moment fleeing as if for his life from yet another obsessed, frantic, wildly-gesticulating woman, her grey hair wild and dishevelled all about her, bleached to a pale no-colour under the harsh strip-lighting of the dim, carpeted corridors . . . . A man in such case might, for one fatal fraction of a second, feel his heart stand still with shock; his brain reel at the impact of a long-forgotten image. His love, his goddess of long ago; the woman who had hypnotised his tongue-tied adolescence with her beauty; and with the brilliance of her intellect had guided him, nurtured him, and launched him on the path to fame . . . here, in the black, rainy night, she was back again at last: back in all her power and her glory, once more hunting him down; an avenging Fury now, dim hair flying, seeking retribution for the long years of indifference and of love betrayed . . . .

*

And of course it had been a shock for Robin, too; must have been. Having so gleefully dumped the burden of his mother back where (in his view) it belonged, it must have been disconcerting to find that sudden death had entered the picture. Now there'd be a whole lot of goddam enquiries, bound to be. They'd be nosing into everything. Was it a crime to dump your ageing mother, just out of hospital, in the middle of a strange city all by herself? Actually, the old girl had been tickled pink at the idea of going to her ex-husband's lecture and scaring the pants off him by popping up in the middle of the audience . . . it was just rotten bad luck that after all they wouldn't let her in. He, Robin, couldn't be blamed for that.

He would be, though. Sudden death made people unreasonable. 'Culpable negligence' they'd call it, or something of the sort; and even if it didn't rate a prison sentence, the whole thing would be bound to land him in trouble of one sort or another. Best, then, to deny the whole thing—surely his word would stand up well against that of a rambling old lady just out of a mental hospital?—and to make assurance doubly sure, he'd get that boyfriend of Piggy's—'Teri' wasn't it, or some such idiotic name?—to fix an alibi. He was reputed to be clever at that sort of thing.

And clever he proved to be. By attentive comparison of newspapers and police reports, Teri soon cottoned-on to the fact that someone was lying about something. First, this stepmother woman swearing that her husband was alive and well all through Sunday . . . and then, on top of that, swearing that her stepson Robin had been at home on the fateful night when Teri knew for a fact that he hadn't . . . this multiplicity of alibis was intriguing, and set Teri's mind toying with thoughts of blackmail (Imogen had been wrong: he did know the word, but was a bit shy about using it). First, though, he needed more facts: and this was where Piggy came in . . . .

*

Meantime, Dot had been writhing silently under her burden of secret guilt.

'. . . And the awful thing was,' she confessed now, 'that the Twickenham house was actually hers, in a way. That is, it was Dad's really, it was in his name, but she'd lived in it most of her married life, and after the divorce as well. Whenever she wasn't in hospital she'd go back there—you realise, don't you, that Minos was her cat to begin with? I thought you might have guessed from his name. She got him for company, when he was a tiny kitten, a year or two before she went into hospital for good—and the amazing thing was, he still seemed to remember her! That was one creature she really did get a welcome from, purring and rubbing his head against her . . . . Oh . . . !'

Here Dot's remorse overcame her once again:

'Oh, I should have welcomed her . . . I should have had her to live with us. But how could I? You don't know what she was like, Imogen . . . . Demanding . . . aggressive . . . and so weird, sometimes, I was quite scared for the children . . . . She kept banging on the door . . . phoning up . . . even letting herself in with her own key sometimes. I kept telling Herbert he should . . .'

So that was what those quarrels about 'Her' had been about—the latter ones, anyway. Not about That Woman at all, but about Lena, and about all the things Herbert could have done about her if he'd been half a man . . . .

'And so we had to do something'—Dot was continuing her defence. 'I mean, it was beginning to break up our marriage, the strain of it all . . . . Our happy, happy marriage . . . .'

She sounded as if she really believed it; and Herbert, from the way he reached out for his wife's hand, seemed to be finding it within the bounds of credibility too. What more could you ask?

'. . . and it was then that I realised we'd just have to sell the house,' Dot was continuing. 'There was nothing else for it. I'm sorry, Imogen, I suppose we should have told you, but I felt so guilty and awful about the whole thing, I just couldn't bear to tell anyone . . . I should have told you, too, about the awful things Piggy was saying about you . . . of course, I knew right from the start that it must have been Mother, not you, raising all that commotion at the hotel . . . but it seemed simpler just to let it ride. I was feeling so awful, you see . . . . Oh, I've been so wicked, so awful . . . ! If only I'd helped her more . . . sympathised more . . . right from the beginning . . . .'

Here it came; the bad memory; the worst one of them all. Imogen had heard it several times already in the last three days, and would hear it again, many times.

Dot, at the age of fourteen, gazing distastefully at the mother she had never really loved, and who was disgusting, now, with alcohol and depression.

'I was appalled . . . she looked so little and hunched, crouching there. She was a big, tall woman really, you know, and always so dignified . . . I hated her for being so small, and so changed . . . really hated her.

"Of course you'll get better," I said impatiently—I was sick to death of the whole thing, you see, and revolted, too—"Of course you'll get better" . . . But even as I spoke, I knew already that whether she recovered or not, I never would. This was the reward of goodness that I saw in front of me, and the long shadow of it would reach to the end of my days . . . .'

*

Dot would cheer up, of course, after the funeral; people do. Also, Robin would no longer be there, the eternally teasing younger brother, deliberately needling his sister. For Robin was flying to Bermuda this very afternoon.

'Didn't I mention it?' he'd remarked, casually, only this morning. 'There's this ex-boyfriend of Cynthia's, you see—no, not the one with prostate trouble; I mean the religious one, who can't divorce his wife unless it should turn out that Cynthia really is getting a sizeable slice of Dad's estate—well, anyway, he's starting up this jewellery business, and he happened to mention in his last letter to Cynthia that he was looking for a bright young man with varied experience—'

'Well, why doesn't he look for one, then?' Imogen had retorted, somewhat tartly—she couldn't help thinking that Robin could have given her some inkling of these plans a bit earlier. 'Your experience isn't varied at all. There's nothing varied about being given the sack, and I'm sure they do it exactly the same way in Bermuda as anywhere else . . . .'

Robin had hugged her, delighted.

'I love you Step!' he'd declared. 'Or I would, if I was capable of loving anyone but myself; but you know what we psycho-paths are!'—and giving her a quick, warm kiss, he was gone.

*

Sitting, now, in the front pew of the icy church, Imogen fan-cied that she could still feel the warmth of it on her cheek, and found herself crying, most becomingly; she felt Edith's approval boring into her from the pew behind.

She would miss Robin terribly—that is if he wasn't sacked and back home again within six weeks flat. But how wonder-ful to be crying, at last, about someone who wasn't Ivor. It was like a sudden, undreamed-of vista as you turn the bend of a mountain after a long, bitter climb; it was like the beginning of spring; the first snowdrop . . . .

'Look, the first snowdrop!' whispered Edith, with appropri-ate melancholy, as they picked their way among the frost-bound graves. 'The first snowdrop of spring—look, Imogen!'

Such was the hushed funereal quality of her voice that Imogen determined to look absolutely anywhere except at the unfortu-nate snowdrop in question. Swivelling her eyes randomly in the opposite direction to the one indicated, she suddenly felt them widen in amazement. There, stumbling towards her between the tombstones, she saw Teri, except that he was only three feet tall and dressed in a pixie-suit. Teri to the life, scowl and all . . . and close behind this apparition, nagging fluently in a clear, ringing tone came Margot, its mother . . . Margot of the coarse black hair; and this—yes, this was the yellow, scowling baby that Imogen had so feared might be Ivor's grandson . . . .

And it wasn't! It wasn't! She nearly executed a little dance of sheer delight behind the coffin.

Good old Robin! Evidently, he'd got himself off to Bermuda just in time. Because, of course, women like Margot don't come to an ex-boyfriend's estranged mother's funeral on a freezing January afternoon for nothing.

She wasn't going to get it, though, whatever it was. Not now. Not with that miniature Teri whining and grizzling at her heels. I'll show her, thought Imogen: Let her breathe just one single word about making any more demands on Robin, and I'll . . .

*

The Psychopaths' Moll. I'm doing it again, thought Imogen wryly. Protecting him . . . cushioning him . . . saving him from the consequences of his follies.

'You know what we psychopaths are,' he'd said: but did she? Did anyone? For all the millions of words written on the subject, for all the decades of learned research, did anyone really know?

*

They were born out of their time; that was for sure. You only had to look back quite a little way in history to find Ivor's by the score, by the hundred, all of them hell-bent on that larger-than-life-size ego-trip which used to be known as the Quest for Glory.

Kings, princes, generals, wiping out whole cities, massacring whole populations, to the ecstatic applause of contemporaries and posterity alike. Teenage hoodlums in their shining armour off to the Holy Land to find a bit of aggro. Rome . . . Carthage . . . Babylon . . . back and back, as far as you cared to look, to the Trojan wars and beyond . . . and there they still were. Achilles, Hector, Odysseus and the rest—they'd all have ended up in Broadmoor if they'd lived nowadays, every last man of them.

And Ivor? Ivor hadn't murdered anyone, or sacked any cities. He certainly wasn't as bad as Zeus, or as the God of the Old Testament. Born into an age when the clash of the long spears has been silenced, and the wheels of the chariots are still; when the black blood no longer gushes forth to the greater glory of victim and assailant alike—what place is there, any longer, for such as Ivor?

Glory? Ego-trip? Call it what you like, it was to this thing that Ivor had devoted all his life and all his talents, as did the heroes of old. Deathless glory had been the prize, then as now, and Ivor had sought it single-mindedly in all the ways that present-day society allowed him . . . . Ivor of the glancing helm, careering over the University campus as if it was the Plain of Troy . . . .

*

'Like father, like son,' Robin had once said to her, implying that his father's glowing success had all been phoney; but this wasn't the answer, either. All over the world, there were men and women who owed their successful careers to the faith they'd thought Ivor had had in them; people whose lives had been enriched and illumined by what they had imagined to be his friendship. Walking the earth this very January afternoon were grown men, alive and well, who, in their long-past student days, had been saved from suicide and despair by what they took for Ivor's sympathy and concern.

What can you say of such a man? What conclusion can you reach about a charlatan whose lies and deceptions have illumined all who came near him?

Well, not quite all. Some, like his first wife, had had their lives wrecked by him.

Or had they? In the end, which of these two was the victim of the tragedy, and which the perpetrator? Ivor, with his callous, arrogant selfishness? Or Lena, the mature, beautiful and brilliant woman who had allowed a foaolish, infatuated boy to tie himself to her for life?

And if, on that wet, treacherous motorway, at one o'clock in the morning, some final answer was given, no living ears were close enough to hear it.

*

After the funeral was over, and the small gathering at Imogen's house had broken up, it was Myrtle who was the last to go. She stood for a minute, uncertainly, at the front gate, sniffing the cold, late air in which, already, there was a hint of spring.

'Darling Ivor,' she murmured softly. 'I'm so glad, Imogen, that you and I, who both loved him, have managed to remain friends.' Sighing, she reached out and plucked idly a bare, brown lilac twig, on which the first faint, pinkish leaf-buds were beginning to show. She turned it this way and that, slowly, between her fingers, and a few tears welled into her eyes.

'Sad! . . . so sad . . . ! You know, Imogen, I think I shall always feel a little bit sad as I pass this particular bit of road: it will always remind me so much of darling Ivor. And of darling, darling Desmond.'

Celia Fremlin:
A Biographical Sketch

Celia Fremlin was born in Kingsbury, Middlesex, on 20 June 1914, to Heaver and Margaret Fremlin. Her father was a doctor, and she spent her childhood in Hertfordshire before going on to study at Oxford. Between 1958 and 1994 she published sixteen novels of suspense and three collections of stories, highly acclaimed in their day. Sadly, Fremlin's work had largely fallen out of print by the time I discovered her for myself in the mid-1990s. But I was captivated by the elegant, razor-sharp quality of her writing and – as often when one finds an author one is passionate about – keen to learn more about the writer's life. Then, in early 2005, I had the great good fortune of having several conversations with Celia Fremlin's elder daughter Geraldine Goller. Geraldine was a charming woman and I found our discussions enlightening, helping me to understand Celia Fremlin better and to appreciate why she wrote the kind of books she did.

One noteworthy thing I gathered from Geraldine was that her mother (highly academic as a young woman, even before she found her vocation in fiction) was invariably to be found immersed in her latest writing project – to the exclusion, at times, of her family. Geraldine also told me that her mother was notorious within the home for embroidering the truth, and was quite often caught out by her family for telling 'little white lies'. Geraldine, however, read no badness into this trait: she simply put it down to her mother's creative streak, her ability to fabricate new identities for people – even for herself.

Who, then, was the real Celia Fremlin? The short biographies in her books tended to state that she was born in Ryarsh, Kent. Geraldine, however, informed me that her mother was raised in Hertfordshire, where – we know for a fact – she was admitted to Berkhamsted School for Girls in 1923; she studied there until 1933. Ryarsh, then, was perhaps one of those minor fabrications on Fremlin's part. As a fan of hers, was I perturbed by the idea that Fremlin may have practised deceit? Not at all – if anything, it made the author and her works appear even more attractive and labyrinthine. Here was a middle-class woman who seemed to delight in re-inventing herself; and while all writers draw upon their own experiences to some extent, 'reinvention' is the key to any artist's longevity. I can imagine it must have been maddening to live with, but it does suggest Fremlin had a mischievous streak, evident too in her writing. And Fremlin is hardly alone in this habit, even among writers: haven't we all, at one time or another, 'embellished' some part of our lives to make us sound more interesting?

Even as a girl, Celia Fremlin wrote keenly: a talent perhaps inherited from her mother, Margaret, who had herself enjoyed writing plays. By the age of thirteen Celia was publishing poems in the *Chronicle of the Berkhamsted School for Girls*, and in 1930 she was awarded the school's Lady Cooper Prize for 'Best Original Poem', her entry entitled, 'When the World Has Grown Cold' (which could easily have served for one of her later short stories). In her final year at Berkhamsted she became President of the school's inaugural Literary and Debating Society.

She went on to study Classics at Somerville College, Oxford, graduating with a second. Not one to rest on her laurels, she worked concurrently as a charwoman. This youthful experience provided a fascinating lesson for her in studying the class system from different perspectives, and led to her publishing her first non-fiction book, *The Seven Chars of Chelsea*, in 1940. During the war Fremlin served as an air-raid warden and also became involved in the now celebrated Mass Observation project of popular anthropology, founded in 1937 by Tom Harrisson, Charles Madge and Humphrey Jennings, and committed to the study of the everyday lives of ordinary people. Fremlin collaborated with Tom Harrisson on the book *War Factory* (1943), recording the experiences and attitudes of women war workers in a factory outside Malmesbury, Wiltshire, which specialised in making radar equipment.

In 1942, Fremlin married Elia Goller: they would have three children, Nicholas, Geraldine and Sylvia. According to Geraldine, the newlyweds moved to Hampstead, into a 'tall, old house overlooking the Heath itself', and this was where Geraldine and her siblings grew up. Fremlin was by now developing her fiction writing, and she submitted a number of short stories to the likes of *Women's Own*, *Punch* and the *London Mystery Magazine*. However she had to endure a fair number of rejections before, finally, her debut novel was accepted. In a preface to a later Pandora edition of said novel Fremlin wrote:

The original inspiration for this book was my second baby. She was one of those babies who, perfectly content and happy all day, simply don't sleep through the night. Soon after midnight she would wake; and again at half past two; and again at four. As the months went by, I found myself quite distracted by lack of sleep; my eyes would fall shut while I peeled the potatoes or ironed shirts. I remember one night sitting on the bottom step of the stairs, my baby awake and lively in my arms it dawned on me: this is a major human experience, why hasn't someone written about it? It seemed to me that a serious novel should be written with this experience at its centre. Then it occurred to me – why don't I write one?

The baby who bore unknowing witness to Fremlin's epiphany was, of course, Geraldine. It would be some years before Fremlin could actually put pen to paper on this project, but the resulting novel, *The Hours Before Dawn* (1959), went on to win the Edgar Award for Best Crime Novel from the Mystery Writers of America, and remains Fremlin's most famous work.

Thereafter Fremlin wrote at a steady pace, publishing *Uncle Paul* in 1960 and *Seven Lean Years* in 1961. Those first three novels have been classed as 'tales of menace', even 'domestic suspense'. Fremlin took the everyday as her subject and yet, by introducing an atmosphere of unease, she made it extraordinary, fraught with danger. She succeeded in chilling and thrilling her readers without spilling so much as a drop of blood. However, there is a persistent threat of harm that pervades Fremlin's writing and she excels at creating a claustrophobic tension in 'normal' households. This scenario was her métier and one she revisited in many novels. Fremlin once commented that her favourite pastimes were gossip, 'talking shop' and any kind of argument about anything. We might suppose that it was through these enthusiasms that she gleaned the ideas that grew into her books. Reading them it is clear that the mundane minutiae of domesticity fascinated her. Moreover, *The Hours Before Dawn* and *The Trouble-Makers* have a special concern with the societal/peer-group systems that adjudge whether or not a woman is rated a 'good wife' and 'good mother'.

*

By 1968 Celia Fremlin had established herself as a published author. But this was to be a year for the Goller family in which tragedy followed hard upon tragedy. Their youngest daughter Sylvia committed suicide, aged nineteen. A month later Fremlin's husband Elia killed himself. In the wake of these catastrophes Fremlin relocated to Geneva for a year.

In 1969 she published a novel entitled *Possession*. The manuscript had been delivered to Gollancz before the terrible events of 1968, but knowing of those circumstances in approaching *Possession* today makes for chilling reading, since incidents in the novel appear to mirror Fremlin's life at that time. It is one of her most absorbing and terrifying productions. Aside from the short-story collection *Don't Go to Sleep in the Dark* (1970) Fremlin did not publish again until *Appointment With Yesterday* (1972), subsequently a popular title amongst her body of work. The novel deals with a woman who has changed her identity:

a recurrent theme, and one with which Fremlin may have identified most acutely in the aftermath of her terrible dual bereavements. *The Long Shadow* (1975) makes use of the knowledge of the Classics she acquired at Oxford; its main character, Imogen, is newly widowed. Again, we might suppose this was Fremlin's way of processing, through fictions, the trials she had suffered in her own life.

Fremlin lived on in Hampstead and married her second husband, Leslie Minchin, in 1985. The couple remained together until his death in 1999. She collaborated with Minchin on a book of poetry called *Duet in Verse* which appeared in 1996. Her last published novel was *King of the World* (1994). Geraldine believed that her mother's earlier work was her best, but I feel that this final novel, too, has its merits. Fremlin marvellously describes a woman who has been transformed from a dowdy, put-upon frump to an attractive woman of stature. The reason Fremlin gives for this seems to me revealing: 'Disaster itself, of course. However much a disaster sweeps away, it also inevitably leaves a slate clean.'

Though Geraldine did not admit as much to me, she did allude to having had a somewhat mixed relationship with her mother. This, in a way, explained to me the recurrence of the theme of mother–daughter relations explored in many of Fremlin's novels, from *Uncle Paul*, *Prisoner's Base* and *Possession* right up to her penultimate novel *The Echoing Stones* (1993). One wonders whether Fremlin hoped that the fictional exploration of this theme might help her to attain a better understanding of it in life. Thankfully, as they got older and Celia moved to Bristol to be nearer Geraldine, both women managed finally to find some common ground and discovered a mutual respect for each other. Celia Fremlin was, in the end, pre-deceased by all three of her children. She died herself in 2009.

To revisit the Celia Fremlin *oeuvre* now is to see authentic snapshots of how people lived at the time of her writing: how they interacted, what values they held. Note how finely Fremlin denotes the relations between child and adult, husband and wife, woman and woman. Every interaction between her characters has a core of truth and should strike a resonant note in any reader. Look carefully for the minute gestures that can have devastating consequences. Watch as the four walls of your comforting home can be turned into walls of a prison. Above all, enjoy feeling unsettled as Fremlin's words push down on you, making you feel just as claustrophobic as her characters as they confront their fates. Fremlin was a superb writer who has always enjoyed a core of diehard fans and yet, despite her Edgar Award success, was not to achieve the readership she deserved. As Faber Finds now reissue her complete works, now is the time to correct that.

Chris Simmons
www.crimesquad.com

Also by Celia Fremlin

Uncle Paul

Waterstones Thriller of the Month

'A slow-burning chill of a read by a master of suspense.' Janice Hallett

'Sinister, witty and utterly compelling. Fremlin was a genius.' Nicola Upson

The holidays have begun. In a seaside caravan resort, Isabel and her sister, Meg, build sandcastles with the children, navigate deckchair politics, explore the pier's delights, gorge on ice cream in the sun. But their half-sister, Mildred, has returned to a nearby coastal cottage where her husband – the mysterious Uncle Paul – was arrested for the attempted murder of his first wife.

Now, on his release from prison, is Uncle Paul returning for revenge, seeking who betrayed him, uncovering the family's skeletons? Or are all three women letting their nerves get the better of them? Though who really is Meg's new lover? And whose are those footsteps . . . ?

'The grandmother of psycho-domestic noir.' *Sunday Times*

faber

Also by Celia Fremlin

The Hours Before Dawn

Winner of the Edgar Award for best mystery novel

'A lost masterpiece.' Peter Swanson

Louise would give anything – anything – for a good night's sleep. Forget the girls running errant in the garden and bothering the neighbours. Forget her husband who seems oblivious to it all. If the baby would just stop crying, everything would be fine.

Or would it? What if Louise's growing fears about the family's new lodger, who seems to share all of her husband's interests, are real? What could she do, and would anyone even believe her? Maybe, if she could get just get some rest, she'd be able to think straight . . .

'Britain's Patricia Highsmith.' *Sunday Times*

'It grips like grim death.' *The Spectator*

'A sharp, tense, clever novel, still readable and relevant all these years later.' *Literary Review*

'Tightly plotted and admirably concise . . . Expertly ratchets up the tension.' Laura Wilson

faber